"I'm assign[...]

"We're well past being formal when there's no one around, don't you think?" Blakely asked. The man still affected her. His voice alone was the equivalent of whiskey poured over crackling ice.

Dalton was tall, six feet three inches if she had to guess. His hair was just long enough on top to curl. He had a dimpled chin covered by a day's worth of scruff and the most piercing set of intense dark eyes hooded by thick black lashes.

For someone so tall, he was built like a brick house. His biceps were stacked. Greek tragedies could be written in honor of his godlike bod and the carnage left behind when he was done with a relationship.

If he wasn't so damned intelligent, he'd be written off as arm candy.

The way he'd looked at her when she was reunited with her nephew earlier said he had a soft spot and was kind underneath those good looks.

"Point taken," Dalton finally said with a half smile that warmed places in her that didn't need to be focused on.

LONE STAR COUNTRY PROTECTOR

BARB HAN

Harlequin
INTRIGUE

If you purchased this book without a cover you should be aware that this book is stolen property. It was reported as "unsold and destroyed" to the publisher, and neither the author nor the publisher has received any payment for this "stripped book."

All my love to Brandon, Jacob and Tori, my three greatest loves.

To Babe, my hero, for being my best friend, greatest love and my place to call home. I love you with everything that I am.

Harlequin® INTRIGUE™

ISBN-13: 978-1-335-69028-9

Lone Star Country Protector

Copyright © 2025 by Barb Han

All rights reserved. No part of this book may be used or reproduced in any manner whatsoever without written permission.

Without limiting the author's and publisher's exclusive rights, any unauthorized use of this publication to train generative artificial intelligence (AI) technologies is expressly prohibited.

This is a work of fiction. Names, characters, places and incidents are either the product of the author's imagination or are used fictitiously. Any resemblance to actual persons, living or dead, businesses, companies, events or locales is entirely coincidental.

For questions and comments about the quality of this book, please contact us at CustomerService@Harlequin.com.

TM and ® are trademarks of Harlequin Enterprises ULC.

Harlequin Enterprises ULC
22 Adelaide St. West, 41st Floor
Toronto, Ontario M5H 4E3, Canada
www.Harlequin.com

Printed in Lithuania

USA TODAY bestselling author **Barb Han** lives in north Texas with her very own hero-worthy husband, three beautiful children, a spunky golden retriever/standard poodle mix and too many books in her to-read pile. In her downtime, she plays video games and spends much of her time on or around a basketball court. She loves interacting with readers and is grateful for their support. You can reach her at barbhan.com.

Books by Barb Han

Harlequin Intrigue

Marshals of Mesa Point

Ranch Ambush
Bounty Hunted
Captured in West Texas
Escape: Big Bend Canyon
Lone Star Country Protector

The Cowboys of Cider Creek

Rescued by the Rancher
Riding Shotgun
Trapped in Texas
Texas Scandal
Trouble in Texas
Murder in Texas

A Ree and Quint Novel

Undercover Couple
Newlywed Assignment
Eyewitness Man and Wife
Mission Honeymoon

Visit the Author Profile page at Harlequin.com.

CAST OF CHARACTERS

The Honorable Blakely Adamson—This judge delivers judgment on some of the most dangerous criminals. Several are released from prison after a paperwork glitch sets them free and one in particular is hell-bent on revenge. Or is there another threat at play? One Blakely doesn't see coming?

US Marshal Dalton Remington—Can this US marshal keep the judge he's assigned to safe and protect his heart at the same time?

Bethany—Is Blakely's fraternal twin keeping secrets?

Chase—Can Blakely protect the young nephew she adores?

Ski Mask—How long can his identity stay hidden?

Chapter One

"Good game tonight, buddy," Blakely Adamson said with a smile. Her seven-year-old nephew beamed back at her from the back seat, his excitement barely contained.

"I never did that before," he said of his first goal. He'd been kicking the back of her seat for ten minutes, reenacting the game-winning score. Out of nowhere, his mood shifted, the moment of jubilee darkened and his shoulders rounded as he exhaled.

"What's wrong?" Blakely asked, checking on him through the rearview mirror.

"It didn't feel so good when it made the goalie cry," Chase explained, shaking his head with the most somber expression. He had a sensitive side that restored her hope in humanity. The world needed more Chases.

"Remember how you gave him a hug?" she gently reminded. "And asked him over for a playdate after telling him it's just a game?"

Chase's smile came back. Kids' emotions were a roller coaster, but they were also pure. "That made him happy again."

"Yes, it did," she agreed. To be seven years old again and so innocent, unlike the grownups she sentenced to prison terms because they didn't know how to play nice anymore.

"Games are s'posed to be fun," Chase pointed out as she

pulled into her neighborhood. It was dark outside; the season was over now that the final playoff game had been decided.

"I know, buddy," Blakely said. He wasn't wrong.

"I don't want to play soccer again," Chase decided.

"Your mom and dad said it's your decision now that you finished the season," she said as she pulled onto her quiet street in the sleepy suburb just outside of the hustle and bustle of Houston. The peace was one of the things she loved most about this neighborhood. That, and the large shrub-lined front yards.

This was a quiet area. Dog walkers were out in the early mornings, always quick with a wave and a smile as she passed by on her drive to work. She didn't know her neighbors well, but someone always hosted a gathering around the holidays. The moms usually hung together, discussing the local school and teachers while arranging carpools and playdates. The few singles in attendance normally kept close to the food spread or bar setup. Blakely's fraternal twin sister, who also happened to be Chase's mom, would fit right in with the former.

Blakely, on the other hand, would rather nurse a drink while trying to blend in with the wallpaper. She wasn't the social twin. After a long, busy workweek, she much preferred a warm bath, a good book and an even better glass of wine. Unless Chase was sleeping over, like tonight. Then, it was tent forts, Nerf wars and a bone-tired level of exhaustion by the time he finally passed out. As much as she loved having her nephew sleep over, she didn't once dream of becoming a mother. If that made her broken, it was too bad. She had a four-inch scar at her hairline on her forehead to remind her that she didn't do long-term relationships either.

Chase sighed like he'd just been asked to solve the climate crisis. "I know." He sat up even straighter. He'd clearly been contemplating her last statement. "My team needs me."

"I'm sure your friends will understand if you decide not to return," she noted. Her experience with first graders might be limited, but most had the attention span of a gnat, off to the next shiny object in a second without looking back. If they were sad, you knew it. If they were happy, you knew it. She highly doubted any one of them lay awake at night, churning over whether they gave the right answer on a test or the right advice to a buddy, let alone whether their friend stayed on the soccer team.

What would it be like to live in the moment again like kids did so effortlessly?

Blakely couldn't imagine.

A bag of leaves that the landscaper had set out for bulky trash pickup blocked her driveway entrance. Another had been knocked over by the wind, its contents spilled onto the drive. Blakely kept her lights trained on the driveway as she put the gearshift in Park, leaving the engine idling. She'd only be ducking out for a second, so she wasn't worried. Force of habit had her surveying the area anyway.

No movement caught her eye, so she hopped out of the driver's seat, leaving the door wide open in the event she needed to reclaim her seat in a hurry. "Stay here, buddy. I'll be back in a second."

Chase nodded before picking up his Switch and turning his attention to the screen and the Super Mario game whose music she could hum from memory. Needless to say, it was his favorite.

Leaves were strewn in a thick blanket in front of her, but she could deal with that later. Tall trees were one of many things she loved about living here. The HOA rules stated leaves had to be picked up in a timely manner, though her neighbors had never complained about hers to her knowledge.

Blakely bent over to set the bag upright when she glanced back to check on Chase and, once again, scan the area. Her Krav Maga training had taught her to always be observant of her surroundings. But then, so had the reason behind the scar on her forehead.

A split second was all it took for Blakely to pick up the bag to use as a landing for the sharp blade coming at her. A ski-mask-wearing male flew through the air, causing her to scramble backward.

Blakely pushed the bag toward Ski Mask as he slammed into it, thrusting the knife deep into the brown paper. Her headlights practically blinded her as she attempted to twist the heavy bag in order to flip Ski Mask sideways.

The move knocked her off-balance instead as he turned with momentum, pulling her with him. Panic ripped through her. Screaming would only alert Chase, who'd been glued to the screen in the back seat. She could hear the music from his Switch as she landed on her side, her head bouncing on the pavement.

Would Ski Mask run toward Chase if he realized the kid was in the car? Take him?

"What do you want?" Blakely managed to grind out. She couldn't get a good visual on his facial features. With him wearing all black along with a hoodie, she couldn't get a decent physical description either. Could she rip the mask off?

"You!" The voice wasn't familiar, but then it was practically a feral growl. Nothing about it sounded human. That one word spoken directly into her ear sent ripples of fear through her. All hope this was going to be a random mugging vanished. As strange as that may sound, it was better than the alternatives.

Fear that she was about to be killed in front of her nephew—and then what would happen to him?—was a punch to the solar plexus. Like prey in the jaws of an alligator, Blakely drew on all her strength to spin out of Ski Mask's grip.

The move worked, temporarily at least. But Ski Mask reacted with the speed of a cobra strike. In the next second, she was flipped on her back. Ski Mask was on top of her, his thighs pinning her arms to her sides, crushing into her ribs.

In case she lived, she started memorizing details about her assailant. He had to be just shy of six feet tall. Built like an athlete with wide shoulders, straight hips and a slim, muscular figure. Not exactly a body builder, but Ski Mask lifted weights.

The description might not be much, but it was better than nothing.

Blakely bucked her hips, or at least she tried. But Ski Mask was too strong. He drew his arm up. The metal blade glinted in the light from the headlamps. Stabbing someone with a knife was a personal way to kill them. It reeked of hatred and revenge.

With every ounce of strength in her five-foot-seven-inch body, Blakely fought back, convulsing. The move was the equivalent of attempting to break free from a straitjacket. Ski Mask had her locked down and was about to deliver a fatal blow.

"Auntie!" shouted the frightened voice of her nephew.

Ski Mask flinched. He immediately turned toward the noise.

"Run!" Blakely shouted, her heart cracking in half that Chase had to witness his aunt's murder. "Go!"

Except the distraction caused Ski Mask to loosen his grip momentarily. And Blakely seized on the moment.

She bucked and twisted. This time, he flew off. The sound of metal skidding across the pavement meant he'd been disarmed, temporarily at least. The next noise was a guttural groan as she connected her knee to the tender flesh of his inner thigh. Blakely was free from being pinned down.

Popping onto all fours, she scrambled to get out of the attacker's reach a second too late. A hand gripped her ankle with the force of a vise. Blakely bit back a curse as she attempted to kick free.

Another hand came around, squeezing so hard she was shocked her bones didn't shatter. Risking a glance toward the car, a moment of relief washed over her at the sight. It was empty. Chase was gone.

Chase was gone! The reality of her nephew disappearing and the possibility of something else bad happening to him sent white-hot anger roaring through her.

Fighting for her life, she drew all her energy and kicked one of her attacker's hands with her free foot. His grip loosened. But only for a split second. Blakely reached toward the fence, struggling to gain purchase.

Trying to claw away from Ski Mask was futile. His grip wasn't allowing her to go anywhere. She needed to come up with a new plan. *Now.* Before he recovered the knife he was reaching for.

Blakely's leg was like an overstretched rubber band at this point. Rather than resist, she curled her body in a ball the second Ski Mask's attention shifted toward the knife that was inches from his long, outstretched fingers.

Body in a tight circle, she reached for his arm and then dug her fingernails into his wrist. The man hardly flinched, but she wasn't expecting to break free from his grasp. His hands were gloved, and the material from his hoodie kept her from reaching skin. *Or obtaining DNA evidence.* At least the material fibers that were now underneath her fingernails could give investigators something to go on.

Ski Mask's fingers were almost to the knife. Blakely tightened her grasp and then exploded, twisting around once again, scraping the side of her cheek on the pavement.

His grip broke. For a split second, she froze, unable to believe what had just happened. Reality smacked hard. She had to get the hell out of there. After popping up to her feet, she ran as fast as her legs would carry her while screaming one word over and over again…*"Fire!"*

If you wanted help, you had to yell *fire* instead. People were afraid when they heard the word *help*. They hid behind the miniblinds, praying whatever was outside couldn't get them too. They instantly reacted to the word *fire*. They practically ran outside to make sure none of their belongings were in the path. *Help* was useless when you needed it most. The reality of people's survival instincts needing them to stay safe was coded into their DNA.

Half expecting to hear Ski Mask's heavy breathing and footsteps coming up from behind, Blakely pushed her legs until her thighs burned. All those Krav Maga lessons she'd taken over the years had just paid off. The Israel Defense Forces self-defense method was created for dealing with real-life situations, like this. She didn't dare risk glancing backward. A second could give an opponent the advantage.

Porch lights came on one by one as dogs barked over her screams. From the corner of her eye, she saw a front door open.

Blakely cut a sharp left and made a beeline for the opened door, yelling the word repeatedly until she reached the front porch.

Mr. Bowman, a widower, stood there in his slacks and sweater with his forehead wrinkled in concern. His hands were balled into fists on his hips as he studied her. The fact he didn't look behind her said Ski Mask didn't follow her.

She expected to hear the squeal of tires as the perp stole her car, but that didn't happen either.

"Call 911," she managed to say through heaves to Mr. Bowman as she hopped onto his porch, skipping the stairs altogether. "Tell them Judge Adamson was attacked outside her home and her seven-year-old nephew is missing. I need help *now*."

Without questioning, Mr. Bowman did as instructed, leaving his door open as he disappeared into his house. Blakely turned around once she made it to his door and could slip inside, close the door and lock it behind her at a moment's notice. The yard was large and boxed in by hedges that replaced fencing. With the porch light on, she would be able to see anyone coming before they could get to her. And she couldn't go inside without knowing what happened to Chase.

Heart pounding the inside of her ribcage, she struggled to breathe as she continued scanning the yard. There was no sign of her nephew or the perp. Was Chase hiding? Running? The thought of him alone in the dark, scared, was a knife through her chest. Her doors were always locked, so he couldn't have gone inside her home.

Where did you run off to, buddy?

Sirens split the air before she caught her breath. Help was on the way, but no real relief came. With Chase missing, there was no way she could relax. She had to find her nephew before Ski Mask did, if he hadn't already.

Don't go there. Not even hypothetically. It will literally unhinge you.

Mr. Bowman came up behind her, cutting into her little pep talk.

"Do you have a weapon?" she asked the older gentleman. "Hunting rifle? I'd take anything."

"I'm afraid not," he said as he came up beside her. "The wife, rest her soul, wasn't comfortable keeping one around since the grandkids." He stood next to her. "Is that your car running?"

"Yes," she answered, grabbing at her side in an attempt to soothe the ache. "It is."

"I can walk over there with you, if you'd like," Mr. Bowman offered. "Hold on a second."

He disappeared and then returned a few moments later with a fireplace poker, a baseball bat and a flashlight. He showed her the offerings. Mr. Bowman was a former runner who was in his early seventies. His build was slight, but she'd seen him out in his yard helping the landscaping crew spread mulch in his wife's flower beds—beds that he'd kept going since losing her last year. The thirty-plus-pound bags were no joke to carry. Mr. Bowman would have one in each hand. Meaning, he was strong as an ox. She knew a few details of his life since he'd joined her at the food spread during last year's holiday party.

"I'll take the fireplace poker," she said. "Thank you."

He locked up behind them and pocketed his keys, and then she backtracked toward the car with Mr. Bowman a step behind.

Blakely needed to get to her phone. She had to call her sister immediately to inform her of the situation. *If* Ski Mask left her purse, which she doubted.

She couldn't remember the last time she'd said a prayer... elementary school? But that was exactly what she did as she neared her vehicle. She prayed her nephew would return to the scene unharmed too, figuring it couldn't hurt.

Because kidnapping Chase was another reason Ski Mask might have taken off without pursuing her on foot.

An icy chill gripped her spine.

A marked SUV came roaring up, sirens blaring, along with a fleet vehicle from the Marshals Service. Would her nephew realize it was safe to come out of hiding? If that was the case, and she could only hope it was because the thought of Ski Mask taking Chase…

Blakely involuntarily shivered at the thought.

Chase, buddy, where are you?

Chapter Two

Dalton Remington, US marshal, parked on the tree-lined residential street and shut off his vehicle. He'd recognized Adamson's name the second the assignment to protect the judge came down. He'd almost beat the local cop cruiser to the scene since he'd been outside of her neighborhood having dinner alone on his way home from court.

Houston PD exited his vehicle first. Dalton was only a couple steps behind.

Blakely Adamson was a dead ringer for a young Jessica Biel, bangs included. Except that Blakely was even more beautiful, in his opinion. Seeing her again was a jolt. The last time, they'd been arms and legs in a tangle in the sheets during the best weekend of his life. Until they broke the rule they'd agreed on at the outset: no discussion of personal lives. On Sunday morning, before checkout time at the Galveston house rental, she'd asked what he did for a living over breakfast in bed. She'd joked that he had law-enforcement swagger and then followed up by asking if he was Dallas PD because she thought she saw something of his with the logo in the back seat of his car.

His response had sent the covers flying. He'd never seen someone get out of bed and dress so damn fast a firefighter would be jealous.

Blakely had sped off, and that was it. They hadn't exchanged numbers, so he'd left it at that. Disappointed didn't begin to describe his mood after she'd made a beeline for the door. There were a lot of people who refused to date anyone in law enforcement due to the dangerous nature of the job.

Now, he suspected he knew the reason she'd bolted. It wouldn't be considered professional for a judge to date someone from the US Marshals Service, considering he could be assigned to protect her. Though, she didn't look much like a stuffy judge while wearing form-hugging athletic wear. The purple sports shirt that fit like a second skin and coordinated leggings highlighted a body meant for making love slowly on Sundays and breakfasts in bed. He shelved the thought, considering the feeling wasn't mutual.

The temptation to write down her plate number had been strong as she'd driven away weeks ago. Not now. Dalton had never chased anyone. His pride wouldn't allow him to start anytime soon no matter how deep their connection had been.

So deep she couldn't get away from you fast enough, dude!

Blakely's gaze widened as it settled on his face, but panic seemed to win out.

Scanning the area, Dalton didn't like the judge standing on the sidewalk, exposed. There were too many places for a perp to hide, get off a shot with a rifle.

"Let's move this inside," Dalton said to her. No need for introductions, and there was no time for courtesies while she was in danger.

"No," Blakely quickly countered. "I need to call my sister and search for my nephew."

"That's not a good idea," Dalton stated. "Someone assaulted you, and it's my job to keep you safe, Your Honor."

"Blakely," she said, standing her ground. "But you already knew that, Dalton."

After a brief rundown of the situation, Blakely moved to the driver's side of her vehicle and retrieved her cell. She held it up toward Dalton and the officer who identified himself as Roger Nordegren. Normally, Dalton might ask if the man was related to Tiger Woods's ex-wife, but there was a time and place for a sense of humor. This was neither the time nor place.

"There's been a situation, Bethany," Blakely started. He remembered mention of a twin, but something about not identical. "When you get this message, come to my home, okay? Just come here, and I'll explain everything."

She ended the call and turned toward Dalton. "Voice mail," she said as though that explained everything.

He wasn't a parent, but a missing child was unimaginable. His heart went out to the parents and to Blakely, who looked so tense her muscles might snap. Understandable, under the circumstances. He thought about what he'd asked her to do a couple of minutes ago. Bad move. All he had to do was put himself in her situation to realize he'd wasted his breath. He wouldn't go inside either if he had a missing nephew out there, not to mention if that child had been in his care.

"What's your nephew's name?" he asked.

"Chase," she supplied and then gave a quick description as she pulled up a recent photo on her phone. The look of horror on her face along with the pleading in those honey-brown eyes of hers made it impossible to stay frustrated with her for the disappearing act in Galveston a month and a half ago. If he'd known she was a judge back then, he would have taken a hard pass on the fling. First of all, she looked way too young and hot to be a judge in the first place. Since they hadn't exchanged personal information other than their real names, he had no idea how old she was or where she lived. Wasn't that the point of a weekend fling?

But Dalton didn't typically engage in sex-for-sex's-sake encounters. Meeting Blakely had made him believe in twin flames.

Dalton cleared his throat before he tripped down Sentimental Lane. He needed to get over himself and the sting that had come with her rejection to find the missing boy.

"You go east, and I'll take west," Blakely said, pointing in opposite directions.

"No, ma'am," Dalton disagreed. "Until the perp is caught, I'm your shadow."

"I've wasted enough time standing here," she said, grabbing her handbag out of her vehicle.

"Wallet still intact?" he asked, motioning toward the bag.

On a frustrated sigh, she opened it and checked credit cards, ID and cash. "All here."

He had to rule out attempted robbery so they could move on. He glanced over at the beat cop. "You got that, right?"

"Yes, sir," the cop immediately responded before calling in the search for the missing kid and alerting his supervising officer of a perp on the loose.

With not much of a description to go on, locating the perp, let alone identifying him, would be the equivalent of finding a needle in a haystack.

"Your nephew might not be far," he said to Blakely. "He might be too scared to come out of a hiding place."

She nodded as her pulse pounded at the base of her neck. Her dilated pupils and quick, uneven breathing told him an adrenaline rush thumped through her.

"Start looking in the shrubs, okay?" he said to her.

"Got it," she confirmed, immediately moving to the nearest greenery.

"Okay if I stay out here and search?" the older gentleman who'd introduced himself as John Bowman asked.

"We can use all the help we can get," Dalton confirmed. "Why don't you start across the street?"

"Yes, sir," Mr. Bowman said with a salute. Other neighbors came out to see what the commotion was all about. Dalton enlisted them to check their shrubs first, then any other possible hiding place a seven-year-old could squeeze into, including unlocked vehicles or boat tarps.

All told, there were a dozen folks out searching for Chase, who was likely to be scared out of his young mind at this point. He might only respond to his aunt's voice, or not even hers depending on how traumatized he was from witnessing the attack.

Taking a moment to examine the scene while it was fresh, he noted the hole in the lawn-and-leaf bag where a knife had been drilled in. Much of the contents were now strewn all over the driveway. He searched for the knife, but the perp must have been clear-minded enough to pick it up before he disappeared.

The scene itself fit the description of what went down according to Blakely. Setting aside his personal feelings about the judge was something Dalton was good at doing. He shoved them down deep, then locked them there. No need to let those rise to the surface again.

Dalton would handle the protection detail and then move on, no matter how much he wanted to ask what he'd done so wrong that Blakely couldn't get out of his Galveston rental fast enough.

BLAKELY TRIED TO steady her voice as she called out for Chase. Maybe he would feel safe enough to come out if she could manage a calm, soothing tone. The thought of telling Bethany that her son was missing knocked the wind out of Blakely. It was horrific enough that he'd had to witness the attack.

What if Ski Mask got to Chase?

Hot, burning tears welled in her eyes. *No. That didn't happen. Chase ran. He got away in time.*

Panic gripped her with fingers that squeezed so hard her ribs might crack. The simple act of breathing hurt as she dropped down on all fours and crawled along the sidewalk in front of her neighbor's house.

She needed to think like a seven-year-old. And fast.

What did Chase like to do the most? The answer came immediately. *Tents.* He loved to climb in tents or find the smallest hiding places.

The trunk of her sedan? Could he have climbed in from the back seat? Would he know it was possible? Would he figure out how?

She popped to her feet and ran toward her vehicle while jamming her hand inside her handbag in search of the key. Her fingers closed around the key fob. She pressed the third button down, the trunk release. It automatically opened by the time she reached it.

Heart in her throat, she looked inside with a prayer Chase would be curled up playing his Switch—which was missing from the back seat—with the sound on mute.

Nothing.

How was she going to tell her sister that the light of her life was gone? Missing? *Abducted?*

To what end? Revenge?

Ski Mask wanted *her*. Would he kidnap Chase to get back at her?

Bethany, call me back.

Her sister's trust ran so deep that she turned off her phone during date nights. She insisted her husband do the same. International businesses ran twenty-four-seven. Even though her brother-in-law, Greg, had a capable junior manager, Greg felt a responsibility to take calls personally to give the kind of individual service that ensured their customers stayed on with the company. Being the sole breadwinner came at a price, and that cost was long hours and missed time with his wife and child. Greg was a good person, devoted husband and loving father. He was a damn fine brother-in-law too. Greg and Bethany Vendenburg were marriage goals because they made decisions together and worked as a team.

It was a great life for Bethany. At least, it had been.

Stress seemed to be getting to Greg, and he hadn't been himself in recent months. He'd obsessed over making plans for Chase in case something bad happened to either of them. He'd even brought up Blakely and Bethany's parents' unexpected deaths as a reason to get paperwork and finances in order. Cracks had been showing in the marriage for a while now too. A year? Ever since Blakely took the bench?

Bethany chalked it up to having a normal marriage. Said it was common to have ups and downs. That she and Greg were on a "down" cycle, but that it would get better. It was logical. Relationships were tricky, full of potholes and landmines.

Blakely, on the other hand, couldn't see herself being happy in so-called domestic bliss, not even when the relationship was on an upswing. She needed her work and had kept her head down for too many years, sacrificing everything, including a personal life, to give up what she loved doing. Besides, what Bethany and Greg had wasn't realistic for most people. Especially not Blakely. Not with her history.

A noise to her left caught her off guard, startling her. She jumped into a defensive position, ready to defend herself or strike anything that came her way. Realized it was just a rabbit.

She checked her watch. An hour and a half had passed since the attack. *Where are you, buddy? Please come out of hiding. Please.*

Out of the corner of her eye, she noted Dalton kept watch over her no matter where he was. Having someone around who had her back was a foreign feeling at best. Since her parents died in a highway pileup on icy roads, she'd been the one to step into the adulting role. Even while attending college in Arlington at the UT branch there, Blakely had looked after her sister, who attended Texas Tech in Lubbock, where she'd met her future husband.

While Dalton had her back, she could focus her full attention on finding Chase.

But where should she look next?

Other vehicles in driveways?

Backyards?

Dog houses?

Didn't her neighbors have kids and grandkids? Would they have forts outside? Tree houses? Jungle gyms?

Since there were a dozen neighbors or more searching the street, this area was more than covered. She glanced over at Dalton, who immediately picked up on the fact she was about to make a move. His offhand remark six-ish weeks ago about having found his twin flame had scared her then because there'd been some truth to it. Once he told her what he did for a living, she'd bolted. The last thing she needed was a fling showing up in court to protect her. Like now. This was exactly what she'd been trying to avoid. She prized her professional relationships and had no intention of damaging her reputation.

The whole fling caught her off guard anyway because she wasn't into casual sex with someone she barely knew.

Twin flame?

Something had caused her to break all her rules and give in to the overwhelming desire to spend time with this man she'd met. She'd believed him to be law enforcement because of his swagger and the Dallas PD baseball cap in the back seat of his vehicle, so trust came easily. Too easily?

When he'd confirmed his job, she'd run just as fast.

Was she letting her guard down? Because she had a four-inch scar at her hairline and another one under her right arm to remind her relaxing with anyone was a bad idea. Her ex had also taught her that it was impossible to really know anyone. People changed. Sometimes, right in front of your eyes.

Blakely made a beeline for her next-door neighbor's driveway. In this area, backyards were protected by eight-foot wood board-on-board privacy fences. The community was known for it, and it was largely the reason she'd decided to buy her first home here. The neighborhood also had a metal gate with a box code needed to enter. The gate kept out solicitors easily enough. A determined criminal?

Clearly no.

The sense of security of the community had been shattered this evening. Blakely realized how false that sense had been.

Dalton saying she'd picked up a shadow was no joke. The man was a half step behind her almost the second she changed course. He kept a distance, though, allowing her the freedom to search everywhere, including underneath her neighbor's car.

Coming up empty, she moved to the backyard. A jungle gym immediately caught her attention. She bolted toward it, resisting the urge to call out to Chase in case Ski Mask was hiding inside instead. Or had Chase in there with a knife to her nephew's throat.

This outdoor swing set was built log-cabin style with a two-story fort that led to a green slide. A pair of swings were next to the fort.

Blakely's heart skipped a beat at the realization this was exactly the kind of place her nephew would hide.

Movement behind the window on the second story of the fort stopped her cold.

Chase?

Or someone else?

Chapter Three

Dalton drew his weapon as he moved beside Blakely. With a nod, he took the lead. Moving a few steps in front of her and then around to the side, he gave the fort a wide berth. Someone was inside. The last thing he wanted to do was further traumatize the little boy if this was Chase.

However, it was impossible to tell who was hiding inside the second story of the jungle gym. Dalton didn't take chances, and he didn't take anything for granted. Until he knew for certain the person in the fort was a child, he would treat the situation with caution.

Slowly, carefully, he scanned the backyard. There was an eight-foot privacy fence around the wooded area. The tree trunks were thick enough for a person to hide behind. Rather than risk being jumped from behind, Dalton moved from tree to tree with the stealth of a panther hunting prey. There was a dozen, give or take, and he checked each one as well as the canopy to ensure no one had found a way to climb up.

Blakely stayed rooted to her spot while he moved in from the back. She stood to the side of a tree, which would give her cover in the event a knife was thrown her way or the perp she'd dubbed Ski Mask had a gun. A knife, Blakely had noted, was an intimate way of killing someone. You had to get up close and personal, look someone in the eyes as you thrust the blade inside them. Ski Mask had responded to her question, asking what he wanted, with one word. *You.*

The fact she didn't recognize the voice wasn't surprising since Ski Mask had spoken the word in a growl.

As Dalton made it close enough to get a visual of the fort occupant, he noted the shape was that of a boy. He turned his attention toward Blakely, who had been studying his every move, and waved her toward the fort.

She caught on immediately and bolted toward the stairs. "Chase, buddy, it's me. I'm coming up."

The image of Blakely reuniting with the scared-to-death seven-year-old seared into Dalton's heart. The kid launched himself at his aunt, throwing his small arms around her neck before burying his face in her hair. His sobs echoed as Dalton informed the officer the search for Chase could be called off and that he'd been found safe. There was, however, still a perp on the loose in the neighborhood. He urged the officer to tell folks to go back inside and keep their doors locked. He further instructed the officer to tell them to exercise caution as they left their homes and report any suspicious activity immediately.

The officer confirmed the instructions. Then, Dalton reported to his supervisor as he scanned the perimeter, giving Blakely and Chase a few moments of safety and privacy. Watching the two of them stirred feelings inside his chest that he had no idea lurked there. Not yet thirty, he was too young to want a family of his own, in his opinion. He'd never had that pull to get married or have kids. His own father, who'd been a good man by all accounts, died not long after Dalton was born. His mother left the family high and dry. The woman took off after Dalton and his siblings had been dropped off to spend a weekend with their grandparents, and she never looked back. Rumor had it that the "Mother of the Year" was remarried with a teenage son. Why the woman who'd walked away from three young children had decided to give motherhood another go-round was beyond his comprehension.

To avoid passing on those genes, Dalton figured the messy bloodline stopped with him. He had siblings who used to feel the same, until his sister, Julie aka Jules, met Toby anyway. Those two were loved up now, planning a wedding. *A wedding.*

Sounded like the equivalent of being sentenced to life, if you asked Dalton.

He had no idea if Jules's future plans had changed. Now that all three of his cousins had found the loves of their lives—his cousin Abi had also become a stepmother—he figured it was just him and Camden left holding the bag. His brother was the oldest on both sides of the family at thirty-five years old. His cousin Crystal was second oldest at thirty-three. Then came sister Jules at thirty-two, followed by his cousin Duke, who was thirty. Both he and Abi were twenty-eight, pushing twenty-nine. All six of the Remington grandkids had followed their grandfather's footsteps into the US Marshals Service.

All six were devoted to their careers and their family. Each were taking turns holding vigil at the hospital after their grandparents were seriously injured in an accident on the farm road where they lived. Their paint horse ranch was being well tended while they were each in a coma, each fighting for their life. Dalton would take his turn next but kept close tabs on the situation, which could go either way at any moment. He couldn't imagine life without his grandparents after they'd taken him, his siblings and their cousins to raise.

Guilt was a gut punch at not being able to be there for

them now. But it was Jules's turn. She'd wrapped a case and had taken leave. Everyone was taking a turn. Though, no one expected the hospital stay to last this long. Camden could take leave after Dalton's turn.

Blakely climbed down the ladder with her nephew glued to her and joined Dalton. "I need to call my sister but—"

It would be impossible to find her phone let alone manage a call without some help.

"Inside your purse?" he asked. His sister and female cousins had trained him never to touch a woman's handbag without express permission, potentially in writing. Once granted, he was never to dig around for more than what they'd asked for. Under different circumstances, he would crack a smile at the memory. This situation was way too heavy for any levity.

"Yes, please," she said, swiveling her hip so that he could gain access to her personal belongings.

He reached a hand inside, felt around for anything that felt like a phone and clasped his fingers around it to be sure. "Do you need me to make the call and hold it to your ear?"

"Would you mind?" she asked. Even now, her voice was like silk.

He tapped the screen and then held the phone toward her face for ID. A moment later, the screen came to life. "Sister's name?"

"Look at call history," she instructed. "She should be at the top of the list." She paused and waited as he tapped again. "Did she call back?"

"Not yet," he stated before holding the phone to her ear.

Being this close, he heard the call roll into voice mail. He could also smell the floral-citrusy scent that had stayed on the bedsheets and imprinted on his soul that special weekend.

Dalton cleared his throat. Another time. Another place.

He might ask her what the hell he'd done wrong. Now wasn't the time.

"First of all, everything is okay," Blakely started. "Whenever you get this message, call me back or head over to my house. I'm fine. Chase is fine." She paused. "I'll explain everything once you get here."

Blakely turned her attention to Dalton. This close, he could see emotion flash in those honey-browns that said she remembered him and that weekend very well. Thick black lashes hid those intense spun-gold babies as she dropped her gaze.

"Thank you," she said, emotion thick in her tone as she held on to her nephew like they were on the Titanic as it was going down. "I don't know what I would have done if anything…"

Her voice trailed off as Dalton scanned the perimeter once more. "You said in your statement that you grabbed hold of the perp's wrists."

She nodded. "That's right."

"Let's get you home so we can collect evidence," he urged. He didn't like her being out in the open like this even though Ski Mask should be long gone at this point. A smart perp would get out of Dodge to save his own hide. A determined perp would bide his time before returning to finish the job. A deadly perp would come back even more prepared.

The threat might be at bay for now, but professional instinct honed by years of field experience said it wasn't over.

BLAKELY WALKED NEXT door to her home and finished giving her statement while sitting on the couch in her living room. In the meantime, Dalton walked the house, closing blinds and ensuring all windows and doors maintained their integrity and remained locked. The medical examiner paid a visit to collect evidence and swab her nails. She managed to take off her jacket while Chase stayed plastered to her body like a baby gorilla to its mother in the wild.

By the time Dalton joined them, he'd inspected the home inside and out. He'd checked the perimeter and set up surveillance cameras at critical points. What could she say? The marshal came prepared.

They probably needed to have a conversation about what happened in Galveston, but that had to wait until grownups could talk without young ears tuned in to every word. At this rate, though, Chase might just have to fall asleep for that to occur. Even then, he might wake up the second she put him down, much like he'd done as a colicky baby years ago. Blakely remembered well the nights her sister had called bawling, unsure of what to do as she paced the floors. Outside of those weeks of colic, Chase had been an easy baby.

The fact she and Dalton had a fling didn't need to be common knowledge. She would ask for his discretion even though he came across as the kind of person who could take a secret to the grave. The man was honorable, intelligent and drop-dead gorgeous. The term *easy on the eyes* applied in spades. It was followed by *hard on the heart* because a man this tall, dark and ridiculously handsome was no doubt a heartbreaker. Had to be, even though her heart wanted to argue against the idea.

Hearts had a mind of their own. Logic kept her from making the same mistake twice—one that could have cost her life at fifteen. Blakely didn't survive that horrific incident just to dive right back in and make a similar mistake—one that could end differently this time—no matter how many years had passed.

Chase snored against her chest, hugging his Switch to his

chest. She didn't have the heart to move him when he looked so comfortable. What he'd witnessed might leave mental scars. Blakely knew all about those. She had physical ones, too, as reminders. But the emotional scars ran the deepest.

"I hope he's young enough to forget all about this night," she said to Dalton as he took a seat in the chair near the couch.

"Kids are resilient," he said. Was he speaking from personal experience? She had no idea. He wasn't married. She knew that much. Which didn't mean that he wasn't a dad.

Considering they'd spent time intimately with each other, Blakely figured they ought to know something about each other now.

"Have you been assigned to me?" she asked, starting there first.

"Yes," he confirmed before diving into what he'd been up to in order to secure her home. "I set up security cameras with sensors on the perimeter. They'll send an alarm to my phone if something with enough body heat and size to be human enters the property."

"I probably should have done that years ago," she said, wishing she'd thought of it.

"You didn't have a reason until now," he pointed out. "Plus, this neighborhood is quiet. You had no reason to suspect a perp would slip past the gate." His forehead wrinkled as he studied her. Under different circumstances, his expression would have been part adorable, part sexy. Right now, all she could focus on was the close call she'd just had and the fact she'd unknowingly put Chase in danger. "How did you fight him off?"

"Krav Maga training," she admitted with more than a hint of pride.

"That's good training right there," he said with a nod of

appreciation. She didn't need it, but the approval was nice anyway. "And most likely the reason you survived the attack."

An involuntary shiver rocked her body at the last word. Chase stirred but immediately fell back to sleep. Between running around on the soccer field, the chicken nugget dinner the medical examiner had brought for Chase—she made a mental note to thank him for it later—and stress, Chase was out like a light not long after his belly was full. He smelled like grass, dirt and little boy, and she wouldn't have it any other way. Plus, there was no way she would have been able to pry Chase off her long enough for him to take a shower.

As long as he was in her house, though, he was potentially in as much danger as she was. For once, she wished Bethany would break the no-cell-phone-on-date-night rule and check her voice mail.

Sending an officer to her sister's home would freak Bethany out, causing undue stress. Plus, she planned elaborate outings involving tents, camping or hotel rooms sometimes. Blakely wished she'd taken more interest and asked more questions about where Bethany would be tonight. Since Blakely had emergency authorization to make medical decisions for Chase, a precaution no one ever expected to need, her sister had the freedom to do whatever she wanted.

Blakely shifted her gaze to the sex-on-a-stick marshal. "Should we get to know each other a little better, considering..." Her voice trailed off as heat flushed her cheeks.

"I'm assigned to keep you safe, Your Honor," he started.

"We're well past being formal when there's no one around, don't you think?" she asked, trying to let some of her embarrassment roll off. The man still affected her.

His voice alone was the equivalent of whiskey poured over crackling ice.

Dalton was tall, six feet three inches if she had to guess. His hair was just long enough on top to curl. The sides were tighter clipped. Small waves of the blond tips contrasted against dark roots that were almost black. He had a dimpled chin covered by a day's worth of scruff and the most piercing set of intense dark eyes hooded by thick black lashes.

For someone so tall, he was built like a brick house. His biceps were stacked. Greek tragedies could be written in honor of his God-like bod and the carnage left behind when he was done with a relationship.

If he wasn't so damned intelligent, he'd be written off as arm candy. But he *was* smart, so that was out.

The way he'd looked at her when she was reunited with Chase earlier said he had a soft spot and was kind underneath all those intimidating good looks.

"Point taken," Dalton finally said with a half smile that warmed places in her that didn't need to be focused on.

The phone alarm caused both of them to jump. Dalton stared at the screen. "There's a woman walking up to the front door who looks similar to you." He glanced over at Blakely and tilted the phone so she could see the screen.

"That's my sister," she said, immediately standing up and making a beeline for the front door.

The marshal was half a step behind. A trill of awareness skittered across her skin at his closeness.

But she was about to face her sister, so she dismissed it.

Even after the fact, she struggled to find the words to tell her sister that Chase had gone missing for a couple of hours. Those were words no parent wanted to hear and no sister wanted to deliver.

Based on the look on Bethany's face, all hell was about to break loose.

Chapter Four

"Keep your voice down or you'll wake him," Blakely whispered to her sister. She gave a quick rundown of the situation.

Bethany pushed through the door and then marched straight into the family room. Wild brown eyes scanned the space before landing on the sleeping boy.

Bethany couldn't get to her son fast enough. She scooped him up, waking the sleepy boy.

"Mama," Chase said as he wrapped his arms around his mother's neck and buried his face in her hair.

"Where's Greg?" Blakely asked as Dalton leaned against the wall.

"We had a fight," Bethany explained as she clung on to her son like he was a life preserver, and her head was dipping underwater.

"Makes sense why you checked your phone," Blakely reasoned as Dalton watched from the sidelines.

Bethany turned toward the front door and then startled when her gaze landed on Dalton. "Who is this?"

"My name is Dalton Remington," he said before Blakely could. "I work for the US Marshals Service," he added when her forehead wrinkled. "And I'd offer a handshake if yours weren't already full."

Blakely's twin offered a pinched smile before she turned to her sister. "I'm taking Chase home. I'll call you later."

"Why not let him sleep here tonight?" Blakely asked, surprising her sister with the question.

"Is it safe?" Bethany asked.

"Safer than you getting back on the road this late," Blakely pointed out. "Plus, I have new security cameras and a personal bodyguard." She walked over and rubbed Chase's back. "He's already asleep. Why risk waking him when you can put him to bed here?"

"Greg will worry," Bethany countered. And then a spark passed behind her eyes. "Maybe that's not such a bad thing tonight."

"What happened between the two of you?" Blakely asked.

"Nothing," Bethany said, her body stiffening like she was tensing up to protect herself from a physical blow.

Blakely bit down on her bottom lip. "It doesn't sound like nothing."

"We had a fight," Bethany said. "Married couples argue." Her gaze shot toward Dalton. "Are you married?"

"No, ma'am," he said.

Bethany shook her head. "Call me ma'am and I look over my shoulder for my mother."

"She's dead," Blakely said with a hollow cast to her voice that sent a nail through the center of his chest. He was starting to regret the pact they'd made in Galveston not to discuss their personal lives. Now more than ever, he wanted to know more about the off-limits judge.

"Doesn't matter," Bethany said. "You know what I mean."

"Right," Blakely conceded. "It wasn't my intention to be defensive about our parents. Tonight has been hell."

Bethany sighed. "Every worst-case scenario possible slammed into me after I heard your first message. All my thoughts went to something happening to Chase. It never once occurred to me that something might have happened to my big sister." Bethany's tense expression softened. "What happened to your face?"

"Put Chase to bed," Blakely said. "I'll open a bottle of wine."

"Are you sure it's safe to stay here?" Bethany asked before another glance at Dalton, searching for confirmation from a second source. He gave a slight nod as her sister reassured her the home was safer than Fort Knox. Bethany nodded before another glance in Dalton's direction. "I could use a drink." Then, she disappeared up the back stairwell in the kitchen.

He had questions but didn't figure it was his place to ask. So he joined Blakely in the kitchen as she pulled out a bottle of white wine from the fridge. "Can I help?"

"Sure," she conceded like she'd just asked to borrow a thousand dollars, and he'd agreed to be her lender. "Corkscrew is in that drawer over there." She motioned toward the granite island and the row of drawers closest to him. The all-white kitchen somehow managed to come off as modern and welcoming with the touches of green plants instead of sterile. The decor fit Blakely to a T.

Dalton moved over to the drawer and then located the metal opener. Joining Blakely on the other side of the counter, he stood close enough to smell her clean citrus and flowery scent—a scent like none other. But he didn't want to think about her unique traits despite seeing her pulse rise at the base of her throat when their fingers grazed as she handed over the chilled bottle.

"Do you want a glass?" she asked after clearing her throat.

He gave a small headshake, needing to be clear-minded

in case the perp returned tonight. Plus, he didn't need to relax and let his guard down again around Blakely. There was no logical reason to touch that hot stove twice.

Dalton removed the packaging on the wine bottle, revealing the cork.

This close, he was reminded of the four-inch scar hidden behind bangs. Was that part of the reason she'd bolted? There were other scars too. One just under her third rib. He'd smoothed his fingertips along all the markings on her body. But ran into a hard wall when he'd asked how she'd accumulated so many.

Dalton stabbed the pointed end of the corkscrew into the plug and twisted.

She'd muttered something about Krav Maga training, but unless she'd actually served time in the Israeli military, there was no reasonable explanation for her to have this many scars.

His ego tried to convince him that the marks were somehow related to why she'd bolted out the door. Were they?

Or had he done something wrong?

With effort, Dalton freed the cork from the bottle with a *thmp* sound.

"I should probably know what you prefer to drink after..."

"We weren't there to talk about personal habits, remember?" he quipped, wishing he could reel those words back in after seeing the blow they landed. "Hey, sorry. I didn't mean to—"

Blakely stared at him. Her expression stopped him midsentence. "You're right, though. We had an agenda that weekend that had nothing to do with getting to know each other. No use getting twisted up about the past."

"Fresh start?" he asked, hoping she'd accept the verbal peace offering.

Blakely studied him. Those eyes piercing right through him. It took a helluva lot to unnerve Dalton. The judge's accomplishment didn't go unnoticed.

"Okay," she said with reluctance in her voice as she set two wine glasses down in front of him. "Do you mind pouring?" She held up shaky hands. "I have serious doubts about my ability to steady my hands enough to get the wine in the glasses." The moment of vulnerability that flashed behind her eyes shouldn't warm his heart. What the hell did it know? It had him itching to reach out and take her hands in his, offer comfort that wasn't part of this assignment. His mission was to keep the judge safe and alive until the perp was caught.

"Not a problem," he answered. After the glasses were filled, she offered water or juice.

"Water's good," he said, thinking a cold beer would be better. Not an option under the circumstances, but better nonetheless. This also seemed like a good time to pepper her with questions while her sister was upstairs putting Chase to bed.

Blakely nodded as she moved to the cabinet to retrieve a glass. Her hip bumped into him as she passed by. Again, he had to ignore his body's reaction to the beautiful and intelligent judge. "Do you have any idea who might want to harm you?"

"A better question might be who doesn't," she said with a frustrated sigh.

"Are you in a relationship?" he asked. He'd glanced at her ring finger the second he'd seen her again. At one point, he'd half convinced himself she must be married, but that was just his ego coming up with more excuses as to why she couldn't get away from him fast enough.

"No."

"Ended one recently?" he continued as he did his level best to convince himself this line of questioning was for professional purposes only.

Blakely stood at the fridge with her back to him, filling his glass with the waterspout on the door. The water stopped mid-fill. "No." Her voice was low and a little too calm. "Unless you count that weekend."

"Nope," he said a little too quickly. "I don't think it qualifies as more than damn good—"

"He's asleep," Bethany said as she hit the last couple of stairs leading into the kitchen.

Dalton had no idea why Blakely would want to live in a house of this size alone. *Leave it alone, Dalt.* Her reason was her own business. Maybe she intended to start a family soon. Dalton involuntarily shivered at the thought as he joined Blakely at the fridge, fighting the urge to loosen his collar. She handed over the water glass three-quarters of the way full.

For a split second, he thought having a family with someone like her might not be a death sentence.

Hold on there, Dalt. He banished the thought. Not yet thirty years old, he had plenty of time to think about tying the knot in the future. No reason to rush it now, especially because he still lived with the mental scars from his parents.

Had his mother's disappearing act not long after his birth given him mommy issues? He didn't need a psychologist to confirm what he already knew. Yes. Being rejected by your mother not long after you were born did that to a person. Not to mention the fact she never once looked back. The woman could be dead for all he knew. One thing was certain. There was no reason to continue those bad genes or dump them on some unsuspecting kiddo. Dalton's father might have been a good person. Hell, Dalton had been too young to make the determination himself, so he relied on his siblings and cousins. They were convinced the man was close to sainthood. Dalton hoped it was true for their sakes. As for him? He'd learned to depend on himself so he didn't and wouldn't need anyone else.

"Good," Blakely said, clearing her throat. It was then he realized she'd been watching him while he'd been lost in thought. "He's been through a lot tonight. I hope the whole thing doesn't leave too many scars."

Dalton knew about those. Too well?

BLAKELY COULD FEEL her cheeks turn crimson as she looked at Dalton, so she forced her gaze from the gorgeous lawman standing in her kitchen and refocused on her sister.

"I know whatever happened isn't your fault," her sister said, cutting into her thoughts. "So please, start from the beginning and tell me exactly what I'm dealing with here."

Blakely gave the elevator version of the attack.

"Ohmygod, Blakely." Her sister cut across the kitchen and wrapped her arms around her. "I'm so sorry. All I thought about was Chase. I didn't even consider how awful this whole attack must have been for you."

Bethany's body was shaking.

"You must have been terrified," her sister continued. "Especially after all you've been through."

Blakely cleared her throat a little louder this time as she hugged her sister. "The past is the past. We don't need to get into any of that now." But it was too late. The hunk of a marshal stood halfway across the room, his gaze fixed on her, questions dancing in his eyes. "Besides, I'm much more worried about the impact this might have on Chase."

"Kids are more resilient than we give them credit for sometimes," Bethany said in a moment of wisdom beyond her years. Her sister could come across as borderline ditzy at times, but then she would say something profound, revealing a deeper side to her.

"That might be true," Blakely conceded, not ready to let herself off the hook for the whole ordeal. "But I hate the fact I couldn't protect him." She couldn't go there with questions about what might have happened to Chase if she hadn't fought off her attacker.

"Both of you are safe, and that's all that matters," Bethany said before taking a pull of wine. She studied the rim. "Family is the most important thing." There was a depth to those words too, along with a hint of desperation.

What was that about?

Blakely remembered the fight her sister said she'd had with her husband, Greg. "Is everything okay on the home front?"

Another long pull instead of a verbal response told Blakely everything she needed to know.

"Tell me what happened," she said to Bethany.

Her sister's gaze shifted from Blakely to Dalton and back.

Bethany motioned toward the small four-top table in the kitchen next to a window. It was one of Blakely's favorite spots for drinking coffee on the weekend. She liked to look out at the tall trees and think. "Mind if we sit down first?"

Blakely picked up the still-full wine glass and headed over to the table. A glance out into the darkness of the backyard caused a chill to race down her spine.

"I can turn on the porch light," Dalton offered, like he could read her mind. Then again, the man was experienced at reading body language, so she shouldn't be all that surprised he'd picked up on her apprehension. Especially considering she was pretty sure she'd involuntarily shivered at the cold front making its way down her spine. Then there was the tension in her muscles that made her shoulders feel bunched up as a headache formed at her temples. So, yeah, she wasn't exactly giving off any relaxed vibes.

"Sounds good," she said before thanking him.

Dalton popped his chin up in a quick nod before heading to the back door. He flipped on the light, which helped ease some of Blakely's nerves. Despite all the Krav Maga training over the years, being attacked had still thrown her off-balance emotionally. Frustration nipped that anyone could make her feel helpless or scared or both again.

A small voice in the back of her mind reminded her that the situation would have been so much worse without all the training she had. Where would Chase be now if she hadn't been prepared? She'd responded to the threat quickly and dispatched the enemy. She'd done her job, which was to defend herself.

And yet, a different nagging voice reminded her that Chase had been in danger. He might be scarred for the rest of his life despite the reassurance from Bethany. Kids were resilient. Except she should never have put Chase in the position to be resilient in the first place. For that, she would never forgive herself.

"Earth to Blakely." Bethany snapped her fingers roughly two inches in front of Blakely's face.

"Sorry," she mumbled, tuning back into the present.

"Where did you go just now?"

"To a bad place where I wasn't able to fight off the sonofa—"

"But you were," Bethany soothed. "That's the important thing. Chase is safe. You're safe. There's no use torturing yourself with what might have happened." As much sense as Bethany made, Blakely still couldn't let herself off the hook.

"Hey," her sister continued. "Talk to me."

"I'd rather hear what happened between you and Greg tonight," Blakely said, turning the tables.

The look on Bethany's face said she was about to lie.

Chapter Five

Dalton borrowed a spare key from a hook on the side of the kitchen cabinet, walked outside and locked the door behind him. He made a trip around the perimeter in search of traces that Blakely's attacker had returned now that the crime scene had cooled down. So far, no sign of the twisted individual.

A list was forming in Dalton's mind. He knew that she hadn't broken up with anyone recently or been in fights with friends. The way she'd said the word *friends* made him think she kept a close circle. She didn't strike him as the outgoing type, which was confirmed through her answers. Basically, she worked and spent time with her sister's family.

His mind went over the details of everything he'd heard so far, stopping at the fight that took place between Bethany and her husband. Since the two were together, there was no way the husband could have attacked Blakely. Plus, she very likely would have recognized her brother-in-law. Curiosity had him wanting to know what Bethany and her husband had been fighting about earlier in the evening. The investigator in him wanted to put together a timeline of events. Was it necessary?

That was always the question, wasn't it?

These types of investigations commonly had a couple dozen offshoots. Taking a wrong turn early on could let the trail go cold. Cold cases were the most difficult to close.

There was a reason. A cold trail, lack of resources, not to mention lack of evidence meant perps walked around free to relocate, repeat their crimes or move on to bigger ones.

In this case, the perp told Blakely he wanted *her*. He left her handbag alone. No money was missing. He hadn't tried to steal her vehicle—thankfully, because Chase had been in the back seat. Carjackers had made off with children in similar circumstances. Most were recovered healthy and in one piece, deemed an inconvenience and dropped off at the perp's first opportunity. A small few weren't so lucky. He mentally shook his head at the senseless losses.

His cell buzzed, pulling him back to the situation at hand. After fishing the device out of his pocket, he checked the screen.

His heart skipped a couple of beats the second he realized the message came through on the family group chat. This was, no doubt, an update on their grandparents. Too much time had passed since both his grandparents landed in a coma after an automobile crash for him to expect good news. A tiny sliver of hope was all he had left, and he intended to hang on to it despite the odds of either of them making a meaningful recovery.

Once again, time was the enemy.

After tapping his thumb on the notification and then verifying his identity with the facial recognition software, the long update filled the screen. His sister, Jules, was at the hospital.

According to the message, Grandpa Lor—short for Grandpa Lorenzo—had coded—again!—but was now in stable condition. A fresh wave of guilt for not being in the hospital at Grandpa Lor's side struck like a prize fighter, cracking ribs in the center of Dalton's chest.

A quick mental calculation weighing how miserable he

would be if he took immediate leave, leaving Blakely to fend for herself should her attacker return, versus how miserable he was currently by not being at the hospital, added perspective.

Who did Blakely have to protect her?

A quick thought that she could possibly move in with her sister temporarily until law enforcement could be certain she'd be safe whipped through his mind like a breeze on a spring morning. Leaving her wasn't an option. Bethany and her husband had had a fight. Marriage could be hard. Apparently, so difficult that a woman could leave her children less than a year after giving birth to her third. And then the loss of a wife could break a man to the point he died.

Was that being fair about his parents' situation? Who the hell knew. No one ever talked about his parents. Or, to his knowledge, ever tried to reach out to his mother for her side of the story. *Anyone who could walk out on three young children without looking back already made her statement.*

Fair point.

Dalton shoved the thought deep down inside, into the darkest reaches of his soul, before responding to the text. Do you need me to come?

Those tiny three dots indicating someone else was typing hit the screen.

Not now. Will keep you posted. K?

He typed a response that he would wait until called. Besides, he was up next once this assignment was over.

For now, he would leave the situation with his grandparents alone and deal with his own heavy heart.

K.

Out of the corner of his eye, he caught movement to the left. For a split second, he thought about this being a decoy. However, the initial attack was alone. Signs pointed to the perp being someone who had a grudge against Blakely, an individual. It wasn't likely he would have someone in the wings.

The moment of hesitation shoved aside, Dalton pulled his weapon from his shoulder holster and headed south in the direction of the stirring. Winds kicked up, causing him to question what he saw. Could have been leaves or a piece of debris floating past a tree trunk. Was he chasing thin air?

The snap of branches in the darkness said he was on the right track. Something was out here. What? A stray dog? Could be a coyote. Raccoons were nuisances out here, as were skunks. The last thing he needed was to be sprayed, causing him to stink to high heaven. Bobcats were a danger in these parts despite being in the city.

With the stealth and precision of movement of a jaguar, Dalton made it to the tree line and back fence of Blakely's small property in less than a minute. Whatever had been in her yard—and he was now certain some living creature had been here—was gone. Giving chase meant moving farther away from the residence.

On balance, it was a risk he couldn't take tonight. Not in the dark. Not when the perp might have visited this site multiple times when planning an attack. Rather than continue, he doubled back instead, pulse racing not from exertion but from stress and fear that he'd left the door open for the perp to attack once again.

The fear wasn't rational. But then, fear never was. He knew, on some level, that he hadn't gone far enough for the perp to double back, beat him to the house, break in and still catch Blakely off guard.

Besides, the perp had learned another point tonight. Blakely knew how to defend herself. She might have taken a few hard scrapes and will wake with a sore body and bruises tomorrow, but she'd fought the guy off. She'd escaped.

Would he use a different method now?

A long-distance shot? The thought of her sitting next to the window—a sitting duck—pushed his legs a little faster. By the time he reached the back door, he was breathing hard and his thighs burned.

As suspected, he saw her sitting at the table near the window as he neared the home. At the back door, he quickly entered and then relocked the door behind him.

"You might want to close those blinds," he said as he joined Blakely and her twin.

A look of panic crossed Blakely's features as her skin momentarily paled. "I close those and someone could be standing on the other side without my knowledge." She straightened her back and shoulders, giving her a royal bearing that shouldn't form the word *princess* in his mind. She had an elegant beauty to her when her chin came up in defiance of whatever or whomever stalked her.

Could Dalton keep her safe?

BLAKELY HAD KNOWN Dalton was heading outside to walk the perimeter. She didn't want to cause unnecessary panic. Bethany had drained her wine glass and asked for a refill while explaining that marriages go through ups and downs. However, her eyes told a different story. Bethany might be able to convince others that she wasn't concerned about her relationship, but Blakely could read her sister like the back of her hand. They might not share exact DNA, but they'd lived in the same womb together, and it was clear that her sister had concerns about her husband. Bethany was holding back.

Chase hadn't mentioned anything or seemed different in any way, which was a good sign that he had no idea what was really going on at home. At his age and with his innocence, he would likely blurt out any secrets. Which only proved he didn't know any.

That had to be a good sign. Right?

"They can stay open," Dalton said after a thoughtful pause.

Bethany bit back her third yawn in a matter of a minute.

"Why don't you sleep with me in the main bedroom?" Blakely asked. "When Chase wakes up, it's the first place he'll head anyway."

Bethany drained the rest of her second glass without noticing Blakely still hadn't touched hers. "That's probably a good idea."

"Should I let Greg know you're staying over?" Blakely asked when Bethany stood up and stepped away from her handbag without a second thought.

"Let him worry," she said before heading up the back staircase.

"That doesn't sound good," Dalton said under his breath.

"They had a fight," she said.

"Did she say what about?"

"Well, no," Blakely responded before adding, "but it's not uncommon for a married couple to disagree."

"Exactly the reason I have no intention of ever willingly falling into that trap," he muttered.

"Same," she said quietly. He tilted his head and half smirked. Meaning, he must have heard her. Not that it mattered. Blakely's marital status and views toward the institution had no bearing on the man. They'd had a fling, nothing more.

A little voice in the back of her mind argued against the

idea of "nothing more." Because the sex had been the best of her life, and she'd gone to sleep many nights since only to wake up thinking about how incredible he'd been. How intelligent and funny he'd been. And how easy it had been to let her guard down in a few short hours with the stranger. The term "stranger danger" applied to everyone outside of her inner circle—a circle that had precious few inside. Three, to be exact.

"We should probably get some sleep too," Dalton said, cutting into her thoughts.

She started toward the front door. "I'll see you out."

He didn't follow.

When she turned around to check, her heart gave a little flip at the sight of him. Dalton Remington stood there, leaning against the wall with thick, muscled arms folded across a broad chest. "Good try, Your Honor."

"What are you thinking? That you'll stay the night?" She shook her head. "I thought you were kidding about that."

"No, ma'am."

"I think we're well beyond formalities, Dalton," she snapped, not liking the change in tone.

"That may well be...Blakely," he quipped, not budging from his spot. "But you have a shadow until this ordeal is over." Before she could argue, he shook his head. "Let me do my job. This isn't personal."

Why were those words the equivalent of pinholes in a balloon? Pinholes that let all the air seep out, deflating the party favor.

Shoulders deflated like said balloon, Blakely conceded.

"Try not to look so disappointed that I'll be sleeping under the same roof," he stated, all cavalier. "You might hurt my feelings."

Despite the horrific evening, Blakely laughed.

"That's better," he said with a self-satisfied smile that she wanted to wipe off his face. "See, that doesn't hurt."

"You're not funny," Blakely countered even though she found herself laughing even harder.

Dalton laughed too, and it shouldn't be the sexiest sound she'd heard even though it was just that. Sexy. Dalton was sex in a bucket. He was also dangerous. As it was, her traitorous heart seemed to need the reminder.

A man like Dalton could smash down all the protective walls she'd built over the years. Walls that kept her heart from being shattered. Walls that kept her from having her head beat in. Again. Walls that kept the world out.

Blakely couldn't risk it even though Dalton didn't seem like the kind of person who would raise a hand toward anyone smaller or more vulnerable than him. Somewhere deep inside, her conscious mind registered the fact she'd brought her hand up to her forehead, where her index finger traced the raised skin at her hairline.

No one ever got to make her feel weak and afraid again. But she would be smart and accept Dalton's help. She wasn't handing over her power so much as using all available resources at hand.

The bastard who'd sent her back to that place—even for a few seconds—of being scared and alone wouldn't get away with it.

"Thank you for the offer of help, by the way," she said to Dalton. "There's a blanket and extra pillow in the ottoman. Hope you don't mind sleeping on the couch since my third bedroom has been turned into my home office."

"Fine by me," he said. "Doubt I'll get much sleep anyway."

"Okay," she said before getting out of the room, up the stairs, and as far away from the man as possible. Being in the same room with him alone made her fingers crave the way his hard muscles under silky skin felt.

Blakely cleared the sudden dryness in her throat. By tomorrow, the perp would be long gone or caught, and Dalton would walk out of her life forever.

Why was the thought no different than a stab wound in the heart?

Chapter Six

Dalton slept in fits and starts over the next four hours until sun streamed in through the windows. He rolled out of bed, fired off a couple dozen push-ups, and then headed to the shower after making a quick trip to his truck to retrieve his emergency supply backpack. In it, he kept a change of clothes and a travel kit with toothpaste and a toothbrush, a comb, deodorant. Pretty much all the basic supplies to get him through a night or two on the road if he couldn't get back home. There was a backup weapon inside, just in case.

On the ground floor of Blakely's home sat the living room, kitchen and dining area. A short hallway to the right of the front door led to a full bathroom and a bedroom that, true to her word, had been converted to a home office. The whole downstairs had a comfortable but minimal feel to it. The place was filled with cream-colored furniture with just the right amount of color worked in. He was no decorator and would never claim to be one. But this space felt welcoming. Like it invited you to sit down and get comfortable so you could stay for a while. Unlike its owner, who seemed like she couldn't get him out of her home fast enough. Blakely was a study in contrasts.

Dalton had no patience for someone who spent most of their time pushing him away despite needing him more than ever. Of course, she wouldn't see it that way. The determined set to her chin said she'd rather eat nails than admit she needed a bodyguard. She was also intelligent enough to accept his help, which he appreciated about the good judge. And a growing part of him wanted to know more about her. Where did she grow up? What happened to her parents? Did she have any other living relatives other than her sister and nephew?

Of course, all those questions were off-limits since they didn't help solve who attacked her last night. On the other hand, they weren't totally out of bounds considering this was an investigation. His job might be to act as bodyguard to the judge, but that didn't mean he couldn't put his investigator hat on. Working with Houston PD was out. They wouldn't share information unless they deemed it relevant to protecting Blakely.

A shower and fresh clothes were the best attitude adjustment he could think of after sleeping on the couch. Since Blakely and her sister were upstairs, he didn't figure a little noise in the kitchen would wake them. His stomach growled, reminding him that he'd skipped supper last night, and he needed caffeine to think clearly.

As he moved into the kitchen and flipped on the light, he heard the creak of a floorboard at the top of the staircase. It was windy outside. Might be the wind. Older homes had a language of their own, creaking and groaning with the weather. Then again, this house wasn't too old. Was someone coming down? Blakely?

He checked cabinets until he found a coffee mug. Then moved to the general area of the coffee maker. She had one of those machines that took pods. Wa-la! A colorful carousel filled with pods sat on the opposite side of the black-and-chrome machine. He grabbed a purple pod, popped it into the machine and set the mug underneath the spout. All these pod machines worked pretty much the same. The noise was worse than he anticipated, drowning out the floorboard creaks, the machine hissing as it spit out coffee. He figured this was meant to replicate the coffee shop experience. As long as the coffee didn't taste burnt, he could care less what kind of noise the machine made. His only hope was that he wasn't waking anyone up.

"Hello," a female voice he recognized as Bethany's said.

"Hey," he answered without turning around. "Do you want a cup of coffee?"

"No," she said, sounding half asleep. "Thanks, though. I just came down for water."

"I can make that happen for you," he said, retrieving a glass and filling it with water from the fridge door before she could plop onto a bar chair pushed up to the granite island.

"Thank you," she said after taking the offering.

"I'm a regular barista," he quipped, laughing at his own joke.

Bethany laughed too. Dark circles cradled her eyes. Stress lines were etched into her forehead. She and Blakely looked like sisters. The family resemblance was strong. To his liking, Blakely was the more beautiful twin, but he admitted that he was biased because there was something about her smile—the few times he'd gotten to see it—that sent a tornado whirling around inside his chest.

"Should I know who you are?" Bethany asked, and he realized she'd been studying him as he retrieved his mug and then joined her, standing across the island.

"What makes you ask that question?"

"You seem at home here," she said on a yawn.

"First time," he said before she could spin a yarn in her mind that had him shacking up with her sister. Not that he'd mind all that much. But he couldn't offer anything more than temporary, and Blakely Adamson was not the temporary kind.

"Really?"

"Don't seem so shocked," he teased. "Kitchens all pretty much work the same. It's not hard to figure out where coffee supplies are, or a glass for that matter. Most folks keep them in similar places. Glasses near the dishwasher and coffee supplies on the counter."

"True," she said with a raised eyebrow. "Do you go into a lot of homes in your line of work?"

"I do," he said a little too enthusiastically. If he wanted to convince her that he didn't know Blakely intimately, he needed to calm down. "It's my job to protect judges like your sister when there's a threat present."

Bethany covered a gasp with her hand. "My sister is in real danger, isn't she?"

He gave her a second to let those words sink in because the question was rhetorical. Besides, there was an obvious threat to Blakely. Had she told her sister the perp was specifically after her? He didn't think so because Blakely wouldn't want to worry her sister more than she had to.

"She's been through so much already," Bethany said. "She's a good person too. She doesn't deserve any of what's happened to her."

"The horse-riding incident that left the scar?" he asked, knowing in his heart the explanation had been flimsy at best. He hadn't asked follow-up questions or quizzed her. He'd been in the brain fog that always accompanied being lost in desire. Being with Blakely had felt a whole lot like what he imagined being in love would be like. Couldn't say he would ever let himself go down that road with anyone. Not with his genetic disaster waiting to happen. For a time, he considered only dating single mothers because the pressure to have a kid wouldn't be a constant undercurrent as he approached thirty. Biology took over with many of his dates, and he found himself being assessed as a potential life partner and father material over dinner when he'd barely eaten the first course.

Bethany stared at Dalton. "Is that where she told you the scar came from?"

"Yes," he confirmed.

She clamped her mouth shut as she shook her head. "Then I sure don't want to be the one to tell you any different."

"She's guarded with me," he explained, hoping to gain a better understanding of the reason while he had her sister alone.

"Not just with you," Bethany said without hesitation. "Although, to be honest, she's more relaxed around you than anyone else I've seen." Bethany's face twisted. "In fact, I thought there might be more between the two of you than an assignment."

"No," he said quickly. Too quickly? It would be unprofessional as hell for him to be in a relationship with someone from work. The consequences of a fling with a judge ending badly were…

Already crossed that bridge, dude. Not on purpose. Looking back, the secrecy had been a mistake—a mistake he couldn't bring himself to regret.

Bethany's eyebrow shot up. "You sure about that? Cuz I could have sworn…" She swatted like there was a fly in front of her face. "Never mind. You don't have to answer that. I'm sticking my nose where it doesn't belong, and I'm probably off base anyway. Of course, my sister would be more relaxed with extra security in the house. Makes sense." She heaved a sigh. "It's just that…she deserves a break. You know? Not some random creep attacking her in her driveway." She caught herself again. "This was random, right?"

"It's too early to tell," he said. "Blakely didn't recognize her attacker, which rules out anyone close to her." *Unless... there were others involved.*

"She sends people to prison in her job," Bethany continued. "That has to count for something."

"We're looking into that angle," he confirmed.

"I knew it," Bethany said on another sharp sigh. "She has gone to great lengths to be ready for the next..." Bethany flashed eyes at him. "You know...to be ready." She chose her words carefully, which meant there was a whole lot more to the story with Blakely's forehead scar.

Dalton had a feeling he wasn't going to like the reason any more than he liked the judge being attacked so close to her home. Given this was personal, someone had to have been monitoring her activities. Waiting for the right time to strike.

His ego wanted to blame the source of the scar for the way she'd treated him. An abusive relationship would make her far less trusting of the opposite sex.

Less trusting of him.

BLAKELY HEARD VOICES in the kitchen as she got up for an early morning bathroom break. Considering her sister wasn't in bed next to Blakely, she assumed the low hum was Bethany and Dalton. Should she be worried the two of them were talking? *Yes.* She should get downstairs before Bethany gave Dalton all the details of Blakely's past.

Her sister wouldn't. Would she?

The older twin by a few minutes, Blakely had always been told she was an old soul. She'd always looked out for her sister and thought of her as much younger despite Bethany getting married first and becoming a mother at a young age.

After finishing up in the restroom, Blakely turned toward the stairs and then headed down. She doubted she could go back to sleep now that her mind was spinning.

Downstairs, she joined Bethany and Dalton in the kitchen.

"Coffee?" Dalton asked, looking a little too good standing in her kitchen in jeans and a black long-sleeve T-shirt.

"Yes, please," she said, joining her sister at the granite island.

"How did you sleep?" Bethany asked.

"I heard you snoring," Blakely said with a smile.

"What?" Bethany feigned being offended. "I already told you that I don't snore."

A cell buzzed. Dalton reached for his and fished it out of his jeans pocket. He studied the screen and frowned. "A distressed-looking man who looks to be in his early thirties is about to hit the doorbell."

"Greg?" Bethany asked, but it was more statement than question.

Dalton crossed the room and held his screen toward them. "Is this him?"

Bethany pushed to standing as the doorbell rang. "He better not wake Chase." She gave her sister a look that could freeze a wildfire before stomping into the living room.

"Think we should go with her?" he asked Blakely, who shook her head in response.

Heated arguments between couples were a landmine for any law enforcement officer to walk into. Dalton would keep an ear toward the front door since Bethany admitted to having an argument with her spouse last night.

"Come home with me," the male identified as Greg said in a hushed but urgent tone.

"No," Bethany stated with more than a hint of defiance in her voice. Whatever the two fought about would most likely be considered a major roadblock in their relationship based on the cold freeze in her tone. "Absolutely not, Greg."

"Should we be listening?" Blakely asked in a hushed tone.

"It's a habit from the job," he admitted. "I need to know that your brother-in-law won't do anything to hurt Bethany."

"I highly doubt that G—"

Blakely held up a hand. She checked her phone, ignored a text from her former law professor.

"Actually, I can't afford to take that tact," she said. "I see it too many times in my courtroom as well as my colleagues'. You think you're safe with someone and that you know them inside and out. But you can never truly know someone, can you?" Blakely caught herself before she gave up too much about her past.

"I said no," Bethany said a little more sternly this time. "My sister's awake in the kitchen, and a US marshal is standing with her. I'll get them both if you don't leave right now, Greg."

"We need to talk," he pleaded.

From the corner of her eye, she saw Dalton reach for his weapon.

"That shouldn't be necessary," Blakely said, pushing to standing. She held up a hand, indicating Dalton should wait in the kitchen. The look in his eyes said he was reluctant. His quick nod said he would listen to her.

Good. The last thing this situation needed was more heat. If Dalton came around the corner with his hand on his weapon, the situation could explode. Not that she'd ever seen Greg completely lose his temper, but he had been buried under work and spending a lot of late nights at the office. He'd remarked that having his own company meant he worked all hours and that, at times, he missed his former corporate job that allowed him vacations and weekends off. The dark circles underneath his eyes were punctuation to that sentence. Her heart went out to him. The pregnancy had been unexpected and had blown apart their long-term plan. Bethany was supposed to finish her college degree and work for five to ten years before the two of them started a family. Chase was perfect and definitely worth a change in plans. But Bethany wanted to stay home with her baby, so Greg doubled up on work. Not only did he work a full-time corporate job, but he also started a side business that grew enough for him to quit his day job and focus on his business. The new plan was supposed to reduce his stress and give him more time to be with the family, but owning and running a business meant working more hours. Lesson learned.

Were they fighting about money?

Bethany had a spending habit, drove an expensive luxury sport utility like all the other soccer moms. She'd had her heart set on a big home in the best school district for Chase.

"Hi, Greg." Blakely stepped into view, using a neutral voice.

"Blakely, please, let me come in and talk to my wife," Greg said. He stood just shy of six feet tall with a runner's build. He had sandy-blond hair and cobalt blue eyes. He wasn't Blakely's type, but most would consider him to be good-looking. But right now, his tie was loose around his neck, and he was wearing the same suit from last night.

"That's not a good idea right now, Greg, but I promise Bethany will be ready to talk soon," Blakely soothed. She quickly assessed that Greg was sober despite bloodshot eyes.

They were red from distress and being rubbed, and most likely dry from staying up all night worrying.

Greg had never been *GQ* ready, but he put himself together well under normal circumstances.

"Leave or I'll tell my sister the real reason we're fighting," Bethany said as Blakely slipped her hand in her sister's and squeezed for reassurance. She had no idea what the fight was about, figured it wasn't her business. Her sister and brother-in-law deserved privacy. Plus, Bethany hadn't let on that anything devastating was going on between her and Greg.

Greg looked devastated. "Fine." He raked his fingers through his hair. "Promise you'll hear me out once the initial shock wears off."

Blakely had a bad feeling in the pit of her stomach. This scenario only proved that you never really knew the person you let in your heart. A piece of hers wanted to argue that Dalton would have been different.

Could she trust it?

The short answer…no. And she'd be a fool to let him in.

Chapter Seven

Dalton fixed a cup of coffee for Blakely, keeping close tabs on the conversation going on in the next room in case emotions escalated and he needed to intervene. Blakely was doing a stellar job of bringing calm to the situation. And he learned something else this morning. For reasons he might never know or understand, Blakely Adamson would never trust him.

The reality shouldn't cause a knot to form in his chest or a sense of dread to tighten around him like a vise. What the hell? The weekend he'd spent with her had been filled with great conversation, humor and the best sex of his life. He needed to let it go and move on because she was all business now. Her normal mode?

Easier said than done, buddy. Especially while he was standing in her kitchen, wanting to dig deeper to find out her secrets.

"Please think about what I said last night," Greg said.

"It's time to go," Blakely stated as Bethany returned to the kitchen, looking like she'd just lost her best friend.

Had she?

"You think you know what your life is, and then someone pulls the rug out from underneath your feet," she said, returning to her spot at the granite island. She looked over at Dalton as he set Blakely's coffee mug down where she'd been sitting moments ago.

"Life can throw curveballs," he agreed.

"People!" Bethany smacked the flat of her palm against the hard surface. "People can throw curveballs!"

"Yes, they can," he agreed as she took in a couple of slow, deep breaths. He'd seen her sister do the same thing to calm fried nerves. *Family trait?* A change of subject was in order. "What about your father?"

"What about him?" she asked.

"Are you close?"

"He's gone," Bethany admitted. She went from white-hot anger to normal on her next exhale. "He and my mother have been gone a long time. Car crash." Those words resonated. Too many lives were lost on Texas roadways. I-45, the road connecting Galveston to Houston and on up to Dallas, takes more than its fair share of lives every year.

"I'm sorry to hear that," he said, drawing on as much compassion as he could muster.

Bethany tilted her head to one side. "Looks like you have personal experience. Have you lost someone you loved too?"

"Grandparents," he stated with shame. He'd been in Galveston for work, not play, when he'd spent the weekend with Blakely. He'd been waiting for word because a felon he was tracking was supposed to show up there. Never did. But he couldn't bill the weekend as a total loss. Not when he'd met Blakely instead. Still, shame was a heavy cloud—he'd been having the best time of his life while his grandparents were in comas. Had Blakely provided a much-needed escape from his life? It had been the first time he'd felt anything but numb since hearing about the crash that nearly claimed his beloved grandparents' lives. Still might. "They were driving home and ended up in a single-vehicle accident that left them both in comas."

"Now I'm the one who is sorry," Bethany said with a frown. "Life is unpredictable. I mean, you think you know where it's headed and that you have a handle on it all. Then, boom! Everything you know changes, and you have to decide what steps to take next."

Dalton nodded.

"Forgive the directness of this question, but shouldn't you be with your grandparents right now instead of here?" Bethany asked, then bit down on her bottom lip.

"I have a couple of siblings and three cousins to share the responsibility with," he explained. "We set up a rotation based on who could take leave the fastest. My turn's next."

Bethany studied him. "How many of the five others have taken a turn?"

"Four," he stated.

"And when you take leave, I'm guessing it's at least a few days to a week," she said. "Which means this has been going on for a long time."

"Yes, it has." Too long in his estimation. And then he tuned in to the sound of the door closing in the next room. A couple of beats later, Blakely reappeared in the kitchen and reclaimed her seat next to her sister.

"Tell me about the fight you two had," Blakely said as she studied Dalton first and her sister second. It seemed to dawn on her that she might have interrupted them. "Everything okay in here?"

"Yes, of course," Bethany said. "Dalton here was nice enough to offer to make me a cup of coffee."

"That's right," Dalton said, appreciating the cover. He didn't want to get into his personal life with Blakely right now. There was no need to get personal with her at all now that all her walls had come back up.

Besides, what did he have to offer Blakely other than great sex?

Not much.

A person like her deserved more than he could give. So he wouldn't push the issue or attempt to break down those walls around her heart again.

He finished making the coffee, which wasn't much more than setting a clean cup under the spout, loading a pod and pushing a button. He had a French press at his apartment that he used on his days off. There was something about the routine of loading fresh beans into his hand grinder, heating water and going through the rest of the steps that relaxed him. On workdays, he grabbed a cup from the small coffee shop on the corner on his way into work. On days he was traveling for an assignment, he did the same. It was important to have a day-off ritual that signaled a change in the lineup. Otherwise, the days ran together in a sea of sameness.

Damn. Wasn't he getting philosophical?

"Here you go," he said to Bethany, serving her a fresh cup of coffee. At this rate, he might change his job description to barista.

"What?" Blakely asked, studying him.

He shot a look to indicate he needed more information if he was going to answer her question.

"You just smiled," she said. "And I wanted to know what put it there."

"Internal joke," he said.

"I could use a good laugh," she continued.

"I doubt it would translate," he said.

"Okay," she said with a hint of disappointment in her

tone. He should probably feel bad except that she wasn't the only one who could keep things to herself. "How about food. Is anyone hungry?"

"I doubt I could eat," Bethany said with a frown.

"What about something calm, like yogurt?" Blakely asked her sister, ever the protective one. The fact they were twins struck Dalton as odd since Blakely took on the role of older sister, and Bethany seemed content to be taken care of as the baby of the family.

"I'll try," Bethany conceded.

Blakely served her sister before turning to Dalton. "How about an omelet?"

He remembered the one she'd made for him in Galveston. His mouth watered at the thought of another. "Only if you'll allow me to help."

"You've been serving up coffee," she quipped. "Your job is done." She motioned toward the spot where she'd been sitting moments ago. "Take a load off."

"I'll take a walk around the perimeter instead," he said, thinking whatever he'd chased last night might have returned.

The reminder of them being in danger struck Blakely like a jab. She straightened her back and moved toward the fridge.

He had a few minutes before breakfast would be ready, so he headed out the back way to investigate the commotion from last night more thoroughly. The sun was shining. Wind had enough of a chill to make him wish he'd worn a jacket. He'd be fine. It would take more than cold temperatures to make him turn around. Jogging helped get his blood moving.

Deer tracks didn't surprise him. He backtracked as best as he could.

Found human prints. Large. Men's.

BLAKELY PLATED HALF of the omelet, placing it next to sliced tomato, then walked toward the back door. As she neared, it opened, and Dalton filled its frame. Her heart gave a traitorous flip at seeing him. The wild look in his eyes sent her pulse racing. "What's out there?"

"Footprints," he said. "It was too dark last night to easily pick them up, and I stomped all over a couple when I chased what I thought was a wild animal away from your backyard."

Blakely brought her hand up to cover a gasp. "You didn't mention it last night."

"Didn't see the need," he said.

"Why wouldn't investigators use their flashlights to check the area?"

"My guess is the attack was initially believed to be random," he said. She'd sat on the bench through too many cases where a beat cop missed important evidence to dispute Dalton's reasoning. Instead, she gave a slight nod.

"Come eat before the food gets cold." Blakely never considered herself much of a cook. She could follow a recipe okay. But she wasn't exactly someone who "created" in the kitchen. Most of the time, she ordered prepackaged meals from a service. That way, all she had to do was toss it in the microwave, hit a button and, wa-la, dinner. Omelets on the weekend were a good way to change things up. Most of the time, she cooked them for brunch before curling up with a good book or hitting her playlist. Unless, of course, Chase was sleeping over. Then, the tent forts came out.

Speaking of Chase, she should probably go upstairs and check on him after breakfast.

Dalton sat down and picked up a fork. He stabbed the egg as he took a chunk out of the omelet and then ate it. Was he frustrated?

The man took his job seriously. Was that the only reason protecting her meant so much to him? Her heart wanted their weekend to mean more than casual sex, especially considering she didn't normally go there, and a place down deep said that Dalton was special.

Blakely stood at the island as she ate, far too wound up to sit down. She paced in between bites, considering how someone could have been lurking behind her home without her having the first clue. She'd kept the blinds open so no one could sneak up on her. She hadn't considered how easy it would be to watch her from afar.

Last bite down, she checked her sister's yogurt cup. At least Bethany was able to finish it. Thank heaven for small miracles. Blakely grabbed a banana and peeled it for her sister next as Chase bounded down the stairs. Tufts of his hair stuck up at odd angles in the most adorable way. That kid had her heart in his seven-year-old hands.

"Hey, buddy," Blakely said as Bethany seemed momentarily lost in her own world. Marital trouble had to be the worst.

He made a beeline to his mother after locking on, mumbling something that sounded like, "I'm hungry."

"Do you want eggs or waffles?" Blakely asked.

"Waffles," he said, perking up considerably at the thought of a sugar rush.

"You got it, kiddo," Blakely said before pulling his favorite brand out of the freezer and then popping a pair into the toaster next to the fridge.

Within minutes, Chase was happily perched in his mother's lap while gobbling down the syrup-soaked treat. Blakely poured a glass of milk then set it next to his plate.

Bethany held on to Chase like he was about to disappear into thin air. Her marriage must be in serious trouble. Not once had her sister bailed on a date night with Greg. The man had shown up looking like he needed a shower and a good shave. And the dark circles underneath his eyes said he was either working too hard or worrying too much. This wasn't the time to pry into her sister's marriage. Not with Chase in the room.

But Blakely was curious about what a marriage that looked perfect on the outside could possibly be facing. Whatever it was, it had to be bad to keep Bethany here. She hadn't made a move to go home or even mentioned the possibility.

"Do you want me to pick up a few of your things from home so you can stay over a couple of nights?" Blakely asked, and then received a warning glare from Dalton. She shot him a look right back.

"I can do it," he offered.

"No," Bethany said. "I can borrow anything I need from Blakely." Something between Bethany and Dalton had shifted this morning. A bond?

As strange as it sounded, even to her, they seemed a whole lot more comfortable around each other in a short amount of time. When she really thought about it, the change happened this morning, while she was at the front door with Greg.

"That a real gun?" Chase asked once he'd devoured breakfast. He was all big eyes and smiles now.

"Yes," Dalton responded. "But it comes with great responsibility and isn't meant for small hands."

Chase sighed. "My hands have always been too small. That's why I play soccer. Because I can never catch a football with these." He held up his hands with a look of disappointment that would melt the most ice-encased heart.

"Hands grow just like every other body part," Dalton reassured. His words resonated with her nephew, turning the frown into a contemplative nod.

A growing part of her liked the ease Dalton seemed to feel around the two most important people in Blakely's life. She gave herself a mental headshake before heading down that no-future trail. She would never trust anyone of the opposite sex. That had been stripped from her a long time ago along with her naïve belief that all humans had good in them. During that time in her life, she'd dreamed of becoming a social worker so she could roll up her sleeves and help people with their transformation.

Imagine the disappointment when she learned not everyone had redeeming qualities or wanted to be reformed. Blakely shook off the reverie.

Everyone she cared about was under one roof. Safe.

For now. Those two words haunted her.

Chapter Eight

Breakfast dishes were a team effort, reminding Dalton what it was like to have family around. He'd gotten used to living alone. Too used to it?

After documenting the shoe imprint and filing it with his office, he read the crime scene report from Houston PD looking for nuggets of useful information. The officer on the report had been wet behind the ears, barely in his twenties. Not that Dalton was old at twenty-eight, but the officer had seemed younger than his years. Besides, Dalton had grown up fast and never looked back. Did it have to do with coming from a big family? Probably. That, and growing up on a paint horse ranch where there was no shortage of work. Everyone pitched in. Chores were a way of life growing up in a ranching community.

Dalton had been as wild as a young buck too. His feet rarely saw shoes in the summer unless he was far out on ranch property. When he was bareback on a horse, he didn't see a need for shoes.

Looking back, it was a magical childhood even though he might not have realized it at the time. No. He'd taken it for granted. Like breathing. Walking. Getting out of bed every morning.

His grandparents' conditions reminded him to slow down and take a look around. Was he afraid of what he'd see?

"Can we play?" Chase asked, bringing over a plastic horse that was sized for a Barbie doll.

"I'm afraid I can't right now," Dalton said. He regretted the words the second Chase's shoulders rounded in defeat.

"I get it," the boy said. "You're too busy, just like my dad always says." He turned to walk away.

"Do you have a baseball?" Dalton asked.

Chase spun around, his face lit like a tree on Christmas morning. "Do I?" He bolted upstairs to what was probably his room. Despite his small size, he made quite a racket on the stairs as he ran up then down.

"Outside with that," Blakely warned, pointing out the back door. A second later, she realized that she'd just asked them to stay outside where Chase would be exposed in the open. "Or, maybe just go to your room to play."

Chase let out a disappointed sigh.

"I just don't want anything to get broken in the living room," Blakely explained.

"We should probably listen to your aunt," Dalton said.

"Will you go upstairs with me?" Chase asked, expecting Dalton to bail based on the kid's expression.

"Why not?" Dalton reasoned. "Let's go."

"Yay," Chase said, then chanted all the way up the staircase.

The little boy had a way of wiggling into even the coldest heart.

"ARE YOU GOING to tell me what happened between you and Greg?" Blakely asked her sister as the two moved to the couch and then sat side by side.

"You go first," Bethany countered.

"Not sure I have anything to discuss."

"What really happened last night?" Bethany asked. "Who is he?"

"That's a question for law enforcement on the case," Blakely said. "Believe me, I wish I had an answer."

"Are you going in to work tomorrow?" Bethany asked.

"Why wouldn't I?"

Bethany made eyes at her. "Oh, I don't know. Because you were attacked in your driveway and could have been killed." Her sister's lips formed a thin line. Brackets formed around her mouth. Worry lines etched her forehead.

"I have twenty-four-hour protection," Blakely pointed out. "The chances of the bastard returning, let alone getting to me, are almost nonexistent." It was the crack in the sidewalk that allowed weeds to grow.

"Dalton will be staying over again?"

"Yes," she confirmed. "It's his job, and he pulled the 'lucky' card to protect me." She made air quotes with her fingers when she said the word *lucky*.

"That must be how you guys know each other," Bethany surmised. "I should have guessed. The two of you probably run into each other at the courthouse."

Not really. But Blakely had no plans to tell her sister the two of them hadn't seen each other before the Galveston weekend. Clearly. What were the odds he would pull this assignment?

When you considered her luck, they were high, actually.

"I'm guessing there's no word on a suspect yet," Bethany continued.

"I would have heard something if an arrest had been made," Blakely reassured. Which didn't mean she would necessarily know if the officers had a suspect.

"It's awful to think there's a possibility that I might lose you too," Bethany said.

Blakely put an arm around her younger sister. "I'm not planning on going anywhere." A tear fell, leaving a stain on Blakely's pajama bottoms. "Hey. I'm serious. I'm here, and I don't want you to worry. Okay?"

"You and Chase are all I've got left," Bethany said under her breath.

"Are you and Greg getting a divorce?"

Bethany exhaled a long, slow breath. Didn't speak.

"Okay, you have to tell me what happened with him," Blakely urged.

"He had an affair," she stated before giving in to quiet sobs.

The fact Blakely had just been nice to Greg, comforting him, caused bile to rise in her throat. She should have given him a piece of her mind instead. Once again, she was reminded those closest to you would only end up hurting you in the end.

"I'm so sorry, sweetie," she whispered to her sister as she stroked her hair.

"Someone from work," Bethany said.

"He confessed this to you last night?"

"That would have been better," she said. "But, no, I found out because she texted him while he was in the bathroom." A few sniffles quieted Bethany for several beats. "She was *sexting* him while he was on a date night with his *wife*. How cliché am I now? Married young. Had a child young. Husband cheated. Divorced before thirty-one."

"You two seemed to have it all," Blakely said. "There's nothing wrong with you wanting to believe the fairy tale."

"Except for the fact the traditional fairy tale is as outdated as I feel," Bethany said. "I didn't finish my degree. What kind of job am I going to be able to get to support myself and Chase?"

"Greg will pay child support," Blakely reminded. "He might not have been around for Chase, but Greg loves his son and trusted that you were taking care of Chase's needs. There's no way he'll leave you in a bad situation. Besides, the last time I spoke to him business was thriving."

"Can I trust anything the man says?"

Good question. One Blakely didn't want to touch. "The love you shared with Greg was real. And he obviously doesn't want to lose you. I'm not saying you should forgive him or go back. Those are your decisions, and I'll support you no matter what. But he'll take care of you either way."

"Yeah?" Bethany asked with no sign of hope in her voice. Then, she added, "Who takes care of you?"

Blakely didn't have a good answer to her sister's question. Until recently, she hadn't given it a thought. Milestone birthdays had a way of sneaking up on you. Turning thirty had caused her to assess her life. Career was on track. Actually, she was doing better than she'd expected there. Personal life?

No one had it all. Right?

Except maybe someone like Dalton. The man was sharp, had a sense of humor and looks that could kill.

Thinking about last night, she regretted the last word.

"It doesn't sound like Greg to cheat," Blakely said. How well did she know her brother-in-law?

Bethany shrugged. "People change, I guess." She blew out a breath. "I should have seen it coming. All those late nights at the office, 'working.'" She hooked her fingers in air quotes.

"Did he offer an explanation?" Blakely asked. As awful as this was, it was taking her mind off her own trouble.

"For cheating or working late?"

"Working late," she confirmed.

"There was always an excuse." Bethany leaned her head

to one side, resting it on her fist as she propped her elbow up on the back of the sofa.

"I thought he hired someone to be his right-hand person last year," Blakely continued.

"He did," her sister said. "Except that Greg said he had to be the one to deal with customers to ensure they had a good experience, or they'd take their business elsewhere." Bethany sank into the sofa. "It's probably my fault too. I mean, I kept asking for a bigger house and nicer cars." She tapped her wrist, which held several expensive bracelets. "I loved when he gave me presents." She gasped. "I think I started loving the gifts more than Greg." Another deep breath. "What if I walked him straight into the arms of someone else who would put less pressure on him?"

"You didn't."

"We don't know that," she said, shaking her head for emphasis. "It could be my fault too."

"First of all, I don't like hearing you blame yourself," Blakely said calmly. Relationships were complicated, and she didn't have a leg to stand on personally. But she'd witnessed the deterioration of many once-blissful unions. At least from the outside, the couples seemed happy. "You aren't the one who violated your marriage. Don't let Greg off the hook so easily. He could have talked to you first. Told you how he was feeling. Brought you into the workplace more. I'm sure you would have rolled up your sleeves and pitched in."

"What if I told him that I was too tired when Chase was a baby, so he never asked me again?"

"Again, not exactly your fault," Blakely pointed out. "When Chase had colic, you didn't sleep for what felt like months. You could barely keep your eyes open while we were in the middle of a conversation."

"Funny how Father Time steals your memories," she said.

Some memories stuck with you forever, etched in the scars on your body as much as the ones in your mind.

"Don't tell me you forgot," Blakely teased.

"Honestly, that whole time was a blur," Bethany admitted. "If I didn't have pictures and videos, I wouldn't even remember Chase as an infant."

"Even that fresh-from-the-bath smell?"

"I could never forget that," Bethany said with a rare smile.

"Don't make any decisions about your life or your marriage while you're this tired, okay?"

"That's probably good advice." Bethany bit down on her bottom lip like she used to when they were teenagers and she couldn't decide what to do next. "It's just that I never see going back home and pretending nothing happened."

"I'm not telling you what to do, so don't take this the wrong way," Blakely said. She wasn't sticking up for Greg so much as making sure her sister played this smart. "But couples do work through infidelity."

"I never thought we were just like other couples, though."

If something like this could happen to Bethany and Greg, no one would be immune.

The crack of a bullet split the air. For a half second, she worried Chase had gotten hold of Dalton's gun. *Impossible.* Dalton would not be that careless.

Blakely shoved her sister to the floor and followed, crouching low. She risked a glance. The family room window leading out to the backyard was cracked and had a bullet hole dangerously close to where Blakely's head had been while seated on the couch. Wild shot?

Not a chance.

Blood pressure through the roof, she didn't hear Dalton

until the lock snicked in the front door and then again when he locked it after leaving.

The thought of anything happening to him caused her chest to squeeze as she reached for her cell to call 911.

Blood on her arm sent waves of panic through her as she checked her body to see where she'd been shot.

But it wasn't her.

Bethany.

"Oh no," Blakely said as her sister's body went limp. "Bethany. Stay with me. You're going to be okay." She could scarcely get out the words through blinding tears and the frog in her throat. "Wake up. *Please.*"

Chapter Nine

Dalton couldn't get out of the house fast enough after the gunshot that shocked the hell out of him. *"Hide in the closet until I come back for you,"* he'd said to Chase, tucking him deep into the walk-in. Older homes in Texas were known for their closet space. The fact came in handy when Dalton convinced the boy to find a spot in the very back where no one would find him.

Dalton dismissed the fear that he would be shot and the kid would starve to death before anyone found him. Besides, Blakely knew Chase was upstairs. She would give her life before anything happened to that child.

Right now, Dalton needed to focus all his energy and attention on capturing the shooter. He ran toward the neighbor's house on the left to circle around and, hopefully, not be seen by the perp. Whoever it was, he was determined. Striking again this soon was a sign of his desperation. Bringing the fight to her doorstep sent a strong message… *I can get to you anywhere you are. No place is safe. Not even your home in your gated community.*

That was the problem with gates. They might keep vehicles out, but a determined individual would walk into the community. Probably scale a wall or fence if there was one. So, no, they didn't work. He imagined they kept out folks who handed out flyers, but they weren't the danger.

As he rounded the neighbor's home, a dog barked. Dalton cursed. The noise would draw attention, giving away his location. Worse yet, the killer could be closing in on Blakely's home right now.

Dalton's training kept him from going to a possibly injured person instead of going after a perp. A quick glance into the family room had revealed Blakely and her sister hunkering down. The fact she hadn't called out for help most likely meant they were both fine.

Blakely would also know to immediately call 911.

As he doubled back, deciding to go round the other side of her residence, he heard the first emergency sirens. *That was fast.* Then again, folks didn't spend all this money to live in a protected neighborhood without law enforcement nearby.

A private-security vehicle came blaring up in front of the house as Dalton crossed the front lawn. He didn't have time to reach for his badge without possibly being shot as the for-hire armed security guard hopped out of his vehicle, wedged in the door and yelled, "Stop or I'll shoot!"

"My name is Marshal Remington," Dalton said, both hands high in the air.

"Toss your weapon," the rent-a-cop ordered.

"I'm a US marshal," Dalton continued as the front door swung open.

"He's okay," Blakely shouted. "You got the wrong man."

The security guy offered a quick apology before heading in the direction Blakely urged.

Then Dalton got a good look at her. Saw blood. "Where are you shot?"

"It's Bethany," she said with a vulnerability in her voice that brought out all his protective instincts. "She's unconscious. Help. Please."

"Let's get some pressure on the wound," he said as he

bolted toward the front door. The moment of relief that Blakely wasn't hurt was quickly replaced with the fear a seven-year-old was about to lose his mother.

The vise tightened around Dalton's chest as he ran inside and to Bethany. A dishrag was soaked with blood as it pulsed from the base of her neck on the right side of her body.

"Her pulse is weak," Blakely said as she dropped down beside her sister, who was lying on the carpet, limp.

"Let's get the bleeding under control before we do anything else," he said, taking a spot on the opposite side of Bethany. He put pressure on the wound using the dishcloth.

"I can't lose her." Blakely's voice was low, and there was a quiet desperation that ripped his heart out. "Or Chase." She paused. *"Chase!"* She gasped. "Where is he?"

"Hiding in the back of his closet," Dalton said, hoping the explanation was enough to reassure her that Chase was fine. Just in case, he added, "He'll wait there until I come for him."

"He can't see her like this," she said. "It'll devastate him."

"The bleeding is under control for now," he said to Blakely, who was clearly in a mild state of shock.

A knock at the door followed by the words "Emergency personnel coming inside" was the equivalent of Christmas morning back at the ranch.

"In the family room," Dalton shouted as Blakely practically jumped to her feet before bolting toward the front door.

In the next few seconds, the cavalry arrived. As Bethany was attended to by a pair of EMTs, Dalton disappeared upstairs to check on Chase.

The little boy was hiding, as he was told to, in the far reaches of the closet. He'd stacked a pile of dirty clothes on top of himself for further camouflage. The kiddo was smart and had good survival instincts.

Dalton had been surviving on his own ever since his mother walked out. Would Chase feel those same feelings of shame and abandonment? Wonder what the hell he'd done so wrong that his own mother would turn her back on him?

The vise tightened once again.

"Hey, buddy," Dalton began when Blakely showed up on his heels. "It's safe to come out now."

A shirt flew across the closet as the mound of clothes erupted and the little boy emerged.

"That was fun," Chase stated, chest puffed out, completely unaware of the danger they'd all been in. "Can we do it again?"

"Not right now," Blakely said. "But I promise we'll have more fun later."

Chase brushed himself off and ran into his aunt's arms.

"I have something to tell you," Blakely said. The sight of the two of them was enough to melt the coldest glacier.

"Are we playing another game?" Chase asked, hope in his big eyes.

"No," Blakely hedged. "This is serious, but I want you to know that everything is going to be okay."

Chase's smile faded.

"Your mommy has been in an accident," Blakely said before quickly adding, "She's going to the hospital, where doctors will take good care of her. I don't want you to worry one bit. Okay?" To an adult, those words would be a sign of just how bad the situation was. To a kid, they offered reassurance.

"What happened to Mommy?"

"She got hurt and started bleeding," Blakely explained in

terms a child could understand. She was good with Chase. For a split second, Dalton saw her with their kids.

Hold on there, dude. Getting ahead of yourself. You have never wanted children.

What the hell was up with the vision?

It had to be the thought of losing his grandparents weighing on his mind more than he wanted to admit. Dalton reassured himself daily that they were strong and would pull through this. With each passing day, his resolve faded a little more. Facing losing them wasn't something Dalton was ready to do. Was this his brain's way to force him to face facts?

His grandparents might not make it, which brought up a whole host of feelings.

Cell in hand, he searched for good news from the home front. While he was wishing, he hoped the officers outside would catch the perp. More than anything, he wanted to be able to tell Blakely that she was safe. Chase had already burrowed himself deep inside Dalton's chest. He wanted to deliver the good news that the little boy was out of danger too. As well as Bethany.

Instead, his world was collapsing around him.

DISAPPOINTMENT AND SHAME shrouded Blakely at the fact she hadn't been able to keep her sister safe. At least Chase was safe. *For now.* She hated those two words.

"Can we go see Mommy?" Chase asked.

At a loss for words, Blakely stuttered. "I—um—"

"Think it might be best to let her get some rest so she'll be good and awake when we stop by later," Dalton said, saving the day.

Blakely wasn't normally at a loss for words. She appreciated the save and shot a quick thank-you with her eyes.

The smile he gave her in return caused her stomach to perform a somersault routine. Dalton had a surprisingly calming effect on her despite the electricity charging the air between them. Their chemistry was undeniable.

But chemistry wasn't everything. Bethany and Greg's had been obvious when they were in school. But she hadn't witnessed it for a long time, now that she really thought about it. They'd shifted into parent and business-owner roles, and all the heat was sucked out of their relationship. The thoughts were random at a time like this, but the brain had ideas of its own, bouncing around to different topics. It seemed to be she'd find solutions when she least thought about a situation. Always, the back of her mind was fitting together information bits to explain things she didn't immediately understand.

"Okay," Chase said, his spindly arms wrapped around Blakely's neck as he held on. She patted his back.

"What do you think about going somewhere else to play for a little while?" Dalton asked.

"Where?" A little of Chase's normal spunk laced the question.

"How about we pretend to be policemen?" Dalton said. She saw where he was going with this. They would have to go to the substation to make reports. Plus, it was probably best to get Chase out of the house before he saw the blood on the carpet. Her window was in need of repair before anyone could stay here again.

The thought of someone targeting her...*her home*...sat heavy in her thoughts. The perp wanted to take her out pretty badly if he was willing to come back so soon. Or did he have places set up in and around her home in case the attack didn't go as planned out front? Less than twenty-four hours had passed since the attack in her driveway. The perp had been clear about what he wanted: *"You!"*

Blakely involuntarily shivered at the thought someone could hate her so much they wanted her dead. Facing facts, she realized that being a judge meant locking criminals behind bars. She presided over jury cases. Technically, a jury made the call. However, she was responsible for sentencing. Figuring out who she upset to this degree was her first priority. Could Dalton take her to her chambers so she could look at case history?

The perp must have recently been released. His voice didn't ring any bells, but maybe if her memory was jogged, her brain might be able to fit those pieces together and give her a name. If she was going to die by someone's hands, she deserved to know who the bastard determined to kill her was.

Without another word, Blakely stood at the same time as Dalton. Chase was too old and too proud to be carried around like a baby. He reminded Blakely of the fact often.

Rather than take the back staircase, Blakely headed toward the front of the house to avoid the bloody scene.

"I'll talk to whoever is in charge," Dalton offered. "Do you want to hang out up here or wait for me by the front door?"

"Front door," she decided, wanting to get out of her house as soon as humanly possible. A shot of rage nailed her for feeling unsafe in her own home. She'd made a promise to herself no one ever got to make her feel that way again. *Not for long.*

The bastard might have won this round, but she'd be ready moving forward. First and foremost, she had to figure out what to do with Chase.

Greg.

In all the chaos, she'd forgotten to call Bethany's husband to let him know what happened. With Chase in her arms, there was no way she'd make the call now. Houston PD would deliver the news if she didn't. Could she make the call without alarming Chase or alerting him to the severity of the situation?

One thing was certain, Chase couldn't be around her until the perp was locked behind bars. It was too dangerous. The thought a stray bullet could have struck him instead was another shot to the heart.

Keeping calm was her best defense. So she tucked those thoughts away as she walked down the stairs, holding her nephew's hand. Dalton had gone ahead.

"Thought you might need this," he said, holding out her handbag. "Phone's inside."

"Thank you," she said. "Mind if I take a bathroom break before we head out?" She could explain what she was really doing once they got on the road.

"Not at all," he said. In a surprise move, Chase let go of her hand and grabbed Dalton's instead. The move choked her up a little bit.

"I'll meet you in the truck," she said.

"All right then," Dalton said, acting cool. The catch in his throat said he was affected by the move too.

Blakely excused herself before heading down the hallway to the bathroom. Once inside, she dug her cell out and studied the screen. Tapped her thumb on the side of the device. With any luck, Greg would pick up. If the call rolled into voice mail, she might lose her nerve to deliver the news.

With a deep breath, she located his contact information and made the call.

Greg picked up on the first ring. "Hello?"

"Hey, Greg."

"Bethany isn't returning any of my texts or calls," he said, sounding frazzled. "Is she there?"

"Are you sitting down?" she asked.

"No," he said. "Why? Is it that bad?" Before she could respond, he asked, "Is she leaving me? Because I messed up royally, and I—"

"Slow down, Greg," Blakely said as calmly as she could. How did she tell the man his wife had been shot at her house—a house where his son also spent the night? "I have something important to tell you, and I need you to sit down."

The phone went silent for a moment.

Then came, "Okay, I'm sitting. What is it?"

How did she get him up to speed with everything that had happened in the last twenty-four hours?

Maybe she didn't. Maybe she stuck to the facts about what had just happened.

"Bethany is being taken to the hospital right now," she began.

"What?" The question was rhetorical.

"My life is in danger, and I'm afraid Bethany was caught in the cross fire," she continued in as calm a tone as she could muster. Hearing those words come out of her own mouth was surreal. Was this really happening? "Bethany was shot, Greg."

"Oh dear G—"

"We were able to stem the bleeding until EMTs arrived," she explained. "I can't tell you what her current condition is. Only that she is being taken to Houston General in an ambulance."

"Alone?"

"Yes, for now." Blakely had to stop by the local substation before she could head to the hospital.

"You were there," Greg said, his voice filled with disbelief. "You have to have some idea as to whether or not she's going to make it."

"I'm hoping and praying just as much as you are," Blakely said. "And don't worry about Chase. He's with me."

"All due respect, Blakely, so was my wife." This wasn't the time for Greg to be indignant, but she understood him needing to take his frustration out on someone. "Sorry. I didn't mean that."

"An apology isn't necessary," Blakely reassured. "I know you didn't mean it."

"Still," he said on a sharp sigh. "Are you heading to the hospital?"

"After I stop by the police substation," she said. "What do you want me to do with Chase? Can you take him?" She paused a beat. "I think he'll be safer with his father."

"Yeah, I guess," Greg hedged. Not exactly the response she was hoping for. "The hospital isn't a good place for him, though. I thought maybe he could stay with you or—"

"Never mind," she cut him off, offended that he wouldn't want to comfort his son while the kid's mother was in the hospital. "I'll make arrangements for him." She needed to think because there was no way she could keep him with her and ensure his safety. "Don't worry about it."

"No," Greg decided. "I should be with him. It's just that work is piling up, and I...never mind. I'll take him to the office with me."

"Okay," Blakely said, pensive, before telling him that she'd drop Chase off after a trip to the local substation. Greg had left the details of Chase's life up to Bethany. Still, it was surprising to see how disconnected he'd been with his own son. Had making a living blinded him to what was really important? His family? And how had Blakely missed it?

Easy. Bethany never talked about the cracks in her marriage. From the outside, she had a perfect life.

Blakely should have noticed how much effort it was taking to create the illusion. She might have been able to help.

"I'll swing by the hospital now," Greg said, sounding resigned.

"Why don't we meet there instead?" she offered. "That way, you can stay there as long as possible."

Greg's hesitation wasn't reassuring. Was she being too hard on him?

"See you there?" she asked.

"Okay," he agreed before ending the call.

She left the call with an unsettled feeling.

Chapter Ten

Dalton tapped his thumb on the steering wheel as he waited for Blakely to join them in his truck.

"I play soccer," Chase offered, filling the empty space.

"How's that going for you?" Dalton asked, unsure what the hell to say to a seven-year-old.

"I don't like it when I score and the other team cries," Chase said, like scoring a goal brought down the weight of the world on his shoulders.

"Do you like kicking the ball?" Dalton asked.

"It's okay."

"Have you thought about playing a different sport?" Dalton asked.

"Yeah," Chase admitted without enthusiasm.

"Or an instrument?"

Chase's face lit up. "Like guitar?"

"Sure," Dalton said, unsure if he'd just opened a can of worms. No one would accuse him of being a good parent. Or of being in a position to give advice to a kid. There was a reason he didn't spend much time with anyone under the age of twenty. He didn't have the first idea what to do with them or what to talk about with them. "Why not?"

"That would be awesome," Chase announced. "Do you think I can quit soccer?"

"What does your mother say?"

"That I can do whatever I want after I finish the season," Chase recited.

"Sounds like good advice right there." Dalton wouldn't argue with teaching a kid to follow through on his commitments.

"What about my friends?" Chase asked in earnest. "Won't I be letting them down if I quit?"

"A real friend would want you to be happy," Dalton said after a thoughtful pause. "Would you want your friend to stay on a team if they weren't happy?"

"No, course not," Chase responded. His eyes widened when it dawned on him. "And they wouldn't want me to play if I wasn't happy."

"Real friends will be there no matter what," Dalton said, wondering when the last time he could say that about another human being had been. Growing up, he'd been close with his family. Now, he had the occasional poker night with a few folks from work and not much else.

His life had never felt empty until thinking about it in those terms. Until now.

What was he going to do about it?

Out of the corner of his eye, he saw movement at the front door. Blakely stepped out, looking more beautiful than she had a right to.

After she joined them, he set out for the closest substation.

"What are all the policemen doing at your house, Aunt Blakely?" Chase asked. His innocence deserved protection.

"They're helping," Blakely said without hesitation. "Do you remember how we talked about how important it is to look for the helpers if something goes wrong?"

"Uh-huh," Chase said.

"Your mom had an accident, so a lot of helpers showed

up to take care of her," Blakely explained. Dalton couldn't think of a better way to explain a stressful situation to a kid. She had a knack for parenting whether she realized it or not. An image of her holding their child stamped his thoughts.

Where the hell did that come from?

BLAKELY TOOK A deep breath. After giving statements while Chase played in a witness room and driving to the hospital, she fixed a second cup of coffee while waiting for her brother-in-law to show.

Dalton circled the waiting room a second time in a matter of minutes as they waited for word from the doctor. All they knew so far was that Bethany had lost a lot of blood and was in stable condition. The doctor wanted to speak to Blakely before allowing any visitors. Her mind kept snapping to wishing she could head to her chambers to check out her files. The identity of the bastard determined to kill her must be hiding in those documents.

She flexed and released her fingers a couple of times to work off some of the frustration. No one got to make her afraid anymore. The exception was this sick sonofabitch coming after her sister or nephew. Of that, she was scared beyond reason.

"Hey." Dalton's calm voice, his deep timbre, brought light to the darkest places inside her. "Bethany is going to be fine, and we'll find the bastard responsible if the law doesn't do it for us first."

She glanced over at Chase. "I'm more worried about him right now." Another dark thought struck. "And what if he comes back for Bethany? You heard the person we talked to at the substation. There aren't enough resources to monitor my sister's room twenty-four-seven."

"True," he agreed, and she appreciated him not trying

to Pollyanna the situation. "I'll speak to the floor nurses and see if they'll keep an extra eye on your sister's room."

"Thank you," she said. She'd been planning to do that herself but didn't want to leave Chase in the waiting room until his father arrived. She checked her watch. Where was Greg?

Speaking of her brother-in-law, the man came zipping into the waiting room looking rough. His jeans and a button-down, collared shirt were the only casual things about him as he rushed into the room.

"Daddy," Chase exclaimed.

Blakely was careful to watch their interaction this time, making sure Chase felt comfortable with his father.

Greg shot an apologetic look in Blakely's direction before making a beeline to his son, who met him halfway across the room. Greg knelt down and embraced his son as a woman in her early twenties stood at the door, looking like she'd rather walk on hot coals than enter the room.

Did Greg bring his mistress to pick up his son from the hospital where his wife lay in a bed after being shot?

Blakely walked straight up to the hovering woman. "I'm Blakely Adamson. Bethany's sister."

The large-busted blonde stood a couple of inches shorter than Blakely's five feet seven inches. Her face flushed hot pink, matching her lip tint. "It's good to finally meet you. I work for Greg as his receptionist." Blakely picked up on the fact she'd said *his* instead of *his company's receptionist*.

Was she reading too much into it? Or did Greg bring his affair to the hospital? Because she couldn't imagine him doing that to Bethany, or Chase. It would mean she had no idea who this man was anymore.

"And your name is?" Blakely asked. She wanted a name.

After a pensive glance in Greg's direction, she responded, "Charlotte, but my friends call me Lotte."

I'll bet they do.

Blakely exchanged insincere pleasantries before turning to Greg. "Speak to you in the hall for a minute?"

His lips compressed, forming a thin line. A flicker of something that looked a whole lot like shame passed behind his eyes before he told Chase to stay put while the grownups talked.

Blakely didn't wait for him to finish before walking into the hall to wait for him. Toe tapping on the sterile white tile, she waited near the elevator bank so Charlotte would be out of earshot. The woman stuck to the waiting room door like glue.

"I know what the fight was about," she whispered to Greg as he joined her. "Is that…?"

"No," he defended, but she could see the real answer on his face in the way his eye twitched when he said the word. Clearly, he wasn't ready to admit it, and it wasn't her business.

"I told her to consider forgiving you, Greg." She shot him a glare that could refreeze Antarctica. "Are you going to make me regret it?"

"You did?"

"Why do you sound so surprised?" she asked, planting a fisted hand on her hip.

"I just thought…you and Bethany are so close… I didn't—"

"What? Think I don't count you as family too?" She didn't hide the disappointment and hurt in her voice. "That's where you're wrong. Because I consider you my brother."

"I'm sorry," he said with a wave of shame. "I let everyone down, and I can't make it right."

"Be the husband Bethany deserves, and the father Chase can look up to," she said. "No matter what happens in your marriage. You can still be a good partner and dad."

Red-rimmed eyes stared back at her.

"I'll try," was all he said. She'd never seen him look so beaten down in all the years she'd known him. How had she missed this?

"Call me if you have questions about Chase's schedule, okay?" she asked, figuring he got the point.

"I will," he promised.

"Do you want to wait for the doctor?" she asked after explaining no visitors were allowed yet.

"I better take Chase home," Greg said, once again surprising her. Wouldn't a husband want to see with his own eyes that his wife was going to be okay? Maybe the marriage was dead. Or maybe he couldn't face Bethany.

Either way, Blakely's heart was breaking for her sister. Bethany might have gotten caught up in a big house and driving a fancy car, but she'd loved Greg very much at one time.

Was all love eventually lost?

Greg excused himself, retrieved Chase, and then left with his son and the receptionist as Blakely made her way back into the waiting room.

"I'd hate for my sister to wake up only to find herself alone," Blakely said as she walked over to Dalton.

In a surprise move, he hauled her against his chest and held on to her. As he whispered calm reassurances in her ear, tears trickled down her face. She couldn't remember the last time she had a good cry. Maybe she was overdue. Because the other option, the one where she felt at home in Dalton's arms, wasn't something she was ready to face.

"Do you want to stick around?" he asked.

"I want to," she admitted. "Except that staying here means not making progress on figuring out who is responsible for all this."

"There's no wrong answer," Dalton said, bringing his hand up to cradle the back of her neck as she looked up at him.

The move might have been a mistake, but she couldn't regret it. Her gaze dropped to his lips—kissable, thick lips that broke over straight white teeth when he smiled.

"Would you kiss me?" she asked.

The question barely left her lips before his grazed hers. He feathered kisses on the corners of her mouth, the dimple in her chin, before covering her lips in a kiss that made her understand the term *weak in the knees*. She brought her hands up to his broad shoulders to steady herself against the wave of desire that slammed into her, sending heat swirling in her belly and on the tender skin of her inner thighs.

Bringing her arms up to loop around his neck caused her full breasts to press against a wall of muscle as sensations lit up her body like a pinball machine.

No matter how many days and weeks passed, she hadn't been able to erase Dalton from her thoughts. She'd dreamed of seeing him again. Although, to be fair, not under these circumstances. He was here now, causing her body to hum with anticipation as need welled up, a squall forming in her chest.

A man like Dalton could shred her.

The thought was the equivalent of a bucket of ice water being thrown on her. She pulled back enough to break their lips apart, instantly missing the way his had felt moving against hers.

"I'm sorry," she heard herself say, breathless. "I crossed a line. I shouldn't have done that."

"Am I complaining?" came the response, and she could

feel his smile as it spread sunshine over her. The fact he was breathless too shouldn't make her want him more. But she did. She'd never wanted anyone more than she wanted Dalton Remington right this minute.

Realizing she'd crossed a professional line—though was it, considering they'd already made love?—she took a step back to put some space between them. This close, she couldn't trust her fingertips not to smooth over his chest and back, mapping every muscle and scar, memorizing every curve and line on a perfect body as she had that weekend.

"We should go," she managed to say, clearing her throat to ease some of the dryness.

"Whatever you want," he said.

Tempting. Because she knew exactly what her real answer would be. *Him.* And that was out of the question.

Or was it?

Chapter Eleven

Dalton reached for Blakely's hand and then linked their fingers as they walked out of the hospital after stopping by the nurse's stand. They'd learned that Bethany was resting peacefully and would most likely be out of it for the rest of the night. The update calmed Blakely's nerves about leaving her sister alone at the hospital.

He was scratching his head as to how Greg could have walked out before seeing his wife and why the man would have brought the blonde with him. *Tacky* was the first word that came to mind. Others followed, but he didn't want to focus on those.

Halfway to his truck in the hospital parking lot, he got the prickly-hairs-on-the-back-of-his-neck feeling. The one you get when someone is watching you. A protective arm went around Blakely's shoulders after dropping her hand. He pulled her close so the shooter, if there was one, would have a difficult time figuring out where he stopped and she began.

"What is it?" she asked, going with the flow. She must have realized something was off based on his body language.

Dalton surveyed the area. The sun was high in the sky on a late Sunday afternoon, blinding him when he looked in the direction he felt eyes on them. "A bad feeling."

Blakely froze. "Should we turn around?"

Dalton normally stared danger in the face instead of turning tail. Setting his pride aside, he couldn't risk a shooter watching them with the sun to his back. Rather than risk her safety, he said, "You go inside, and I'll grab the truck."

"Is that safe?" she asked.

"They don't want me," he said.

"What if they decide punishing me is better than killing me?" she asked with a vulnerability in her voice that caused his free hand to fist. She had a point. They had no idea who was doing this and for what reason. Though, he suspected this was someone she'd given the maximum sentence to while seated on the bench.

Until they had answers, she was right to be cautious. Even then, he wanted her to be cautious.

"I'll be careful," he promised before feathering a kiss on her forehead. Suddenly, he realized they were in public, and this wouldn't look professional for either one of them. He cleared his throat and dropped his arm from around her shoulder. "Go inside and wait by the ER doors. Stand behind a big planter. Okay?"

She nodded before turning and heading inside. For a second, he thought she might argue. The woman had an independent streak a mile long. It was one of many traits that made her sexy as all get out to his thinking. Strong women were sexy. Opinionated women were sexy. Intelligent women were sexy.

Blakely had it all.

Dalton stepped into what he guessed would be the line of fire as she doubled back to the hospital. Once she was in a secure location, he dodged in between vehicles on his way to his truck. Made it safely there.

Sliding into the driver's seat, he saw a glint of metal in the direction he'd gotten the heebie-jeebies from a few minutes ago. Keeping a low profile, he hunched down in the seat and then started the engine. Pulling out of the parking space, he half expected bullets to fly. Found himself tensing up in preparation for one of those bullets to break his passenger window and lodge itself into his flesh.

Thankfully, none of that happened as he made his way toward the ER bay and then positioned the truck in front of the glass doors, which opened with a swish. Ducking low, Blakely rushed out without a backward glance.

Again, no bullets flew. He'd take that as a win.

"I'm making a call to the nurse's station to let them know there could be someone out in the parking lot," she said as she lowered the seat until she was flat on her back.

"Good idea," he agreed as he mashed the gas pedal before someone came out and yelled at them for being in the ambulance bay. He didn't mind getting into trouble. Hell, he'd been in trouble most of his childhood. What bothered him was the fact someone could get caught in the crosshairs should this bastard decide to fire.

Shoving those thoughts aside, he navigated out of the parking lot as he double-checked his mirrors to make certain no one followed. Once clear of the hospital, he said, "It's safe to sit up now if you want."

She finished the call and then brought her seat back up. "I feel much better now that the nurses are aware."

"It might have been nothing, but it's better to be safe than sorry," he agreed.

"I hate that I dragged you into this mess," Blakely stated.

"Just doing my job," he said as he pulled up to a red light. Glancing over at Blakely, he added, "And it's a job I happen to love and am damn good at."

The corners of her lips tightened in a frown.

"That, you are," she responded, turning her face away to stare out the passenger-side window. She glanced at the side mirror too. "You've kept me alive so far."

"We make a good team," he said, not loving the fact he'd been the one to make her frown. Something told him that she didn't smile nearly enough.

The rest of the ride to the courthouse was spent in silence. The face of this courthouse wasn't much to look at. It was mostly brick and mortar. Inside, by contrast, it was grander. The courtrooms themselves were smaller than he'd expected on his first visit, but he was used to them now. He'd been inside judges' chambers several times throughout his career, each with the same large mahogany desks. The Texas and American flags flanked leather executive chairs. Every judge had the same green law-library desk lamp. Did it remind them of their college days? When the law was an ideal instead of the reality they carried out every day? A time when most of the people they encountered were still good, instead of the horrors they came across in the courtroom in a defendant's chair?

Blakely's chambers had a wall of books on one side along with a pair of leather chairs that looked comfortable to sit in.

"I hope you understand that I can't let you sit next to me while I scan files for names," she said.

"Right," he said. "Of course. Do you want to talk through the kind of person you might be looking for?"

"I have a few cases in mind where I've forgotten details and names, but faces stick out," she said. "Figured I'd start there and with the ones who sneered at me while I handed down their sentences."

"Seems like a good place to begin," he concurred, taking one of the leather chairs that turned out to be as comfortable as it had looked. His cell buzzed in his pocket. He fished it out and then held it up. "I'll take this while you search."

Blakely's full attention was already on the screen that had come to life, casting a glow on her face in the otherwise dim room. She studied the screen, and he was almost certain she hadn't heard a word he'd said.

His first instinct was the call coming in must be an update about his grandparents. But, no, he didn't recognize the number.

"Hello?"

"Hello, Marshal Remington," the familiar voice said. He'd spoken to the investigator at the scene this morning. "Detective Harvey here."

"Right," Dalton said. Now he had a name to a voice. "How can I help you, Detective?"

"Got a call from Johnny Spear's parole officer a few minutes ago," Harvey said.

"Name doesn't ring a bell," Dalton responded as he watched Blakely scroll through case files. Was this what she had been like in law school? Quiet? Studious? Had she been the nose-always-in-a-book type?

"You might want to ask the judge if she knows it," Harvey continued. "Because there was a paperwork error that led to him being released by mistake."

Dalton lowered the receiver away from his mouth. "Do you know anyone by the name of Johnny Spear?"

Her lips compressed, and she brought her gaze up and to the right. "Sounds familiar. But recent." Her fingers danced across the keyboard. Then, she dropped her gaze to the screen. "Oh, wait. Yes. I do remember him. He is recent. I gave him the maximum sentence for murdering his family. He claimed self-defense against his seventy-year-old father." She looked at Dalton and seemed to realize he still had someone on the line. "Why?"

He held up a finger, telling her to wait.

Had they found their perp?

"HER HONOR KNOWS the individual in question," Dalton supplied as Blakely waited with bated breath. She distinctly remembered the threat he'd made as he was being handcuffed and then taken out of the courtroom by the bailiff. He'd dropped the f-bomb on her, made certain she could see that he was flipping her off despite the restraints and had warned her to watch her back from now on.

She'd taken this as another idle threat. Hardened individuals weren't all that happy with her when she handed down maximum sentences, which she only did when the situation warranted. Keeping honest people safe was the only legitimate reason to take away another person's rights. She didn't take the responsibility lightly. Still. If she had a nickel for every idle threat she received, she would someday be a very wealthy woman.

"I see," Dalton said into the phone. "Okay." He paused a couple of beats. "I'll let the judge know." More silence. "I appreciate the information, Detective."

Blakely had a bad feeling about this.

The second Dalton ended the call, she asked, "What has Johnny Spear done?"

The look on Dalton's face sent her blood pressure rising. "Turns out, he didn't show up for his parole appointment."

"I just sentenced him last month," she said with an arched brow. "He shouldn't be eligible for parole."

"I'm afraid there was a paperwork error," he explained. "Johnny Spear was released last Tuesday."

"He didn't waste a lot of time coming after me," she

said, hearing the shock in her own voice. This wasn't good. Johnny had been clear with his intentions. "Do they have an address on him?"

"I'm afraid he's disappeared," Dalton said. "A BOLO is being issued right now as we speak."

Before she could respond, her cell buzzed. "Hold that thought." She grabbed her cell from her handbag and then checked the screen. "This is the nurse I spoke to earlier. I better take this.

"Is everything okay with Bethany?"

"Yes, sorry to scare you," Nurse Lena said. "There's a man here with flowers who says he's a friend of the family. Since your sister isn't allowed visitors that aren't blood relatives, I denied access to the room."

"Did he give a name?" Blakely asked, thinking this didn't sound so good.

"Dr. Canon," Lena supplied. *What the hell was he doing there?* "I can't let him into my patient's room."

"You did the right thing," Blakely stated, wondering if she should have ignored her former law professor's text this morning.

The nurse's voice dropped to a whisper. "He's standing here right now asking to speak to you. Should I hand him the phone?"

"Absolutely," Blakely stated.

Static came through the line.

"You've been difficult to reach lately, Miss Adamson," Dr. Ellery Canon's familiar voice sounded.

"What are you doing at the hospital?" she asked, ignoring his comment.

"I was worried about you since you haven't returned any of my calls or texts," he said like that should be plain as the nose on her face. "Then, your address came up, and I thought something might have happened to you."

"Oh, right, your scanners," she said, remembering how often he used to mention that scanners could be useful tools for a lawyer. The fact he recognized her address when it came up was just creepy. Blakely remembered overhearing a conversation once between a pair of female students about Dr. Canon. Midterm test results had come back. The front-row students had commented about their A's, saying the rumor was true. All a female student had to do in order to get an A in his criminal law class was to sit in the front row, wear a low-cut blouse and use cleavage to their advantage. They'd said he was harmless enough, and they didn't mind giving the old man a thrill. Even if Blakely wasn't a 34B, she would never have stooped so low to get a grade. For better or worse, she'd earned every single alphabet letter on her grade reports and was proud of the fact.

Still. He'd called her one of his prize students, had invited her along with a few male colleagues to his home for dinners a handful of times since graduation and had been a big cheerleader for her career since she'd left college.

"I brought flowers for you," he said. "But I guess these are for someone else now."

"The nurse can take them," she offered, not wanting to offend her former professor. He still had pull in certain circles, and she'd worked for and deserved a clean reputation. She was still too early in her career to make enemies, and the man had never been inappropriate with her.

"I'll make sure they get to the right place," Blakely offered. "It's not necessary for you to stick around."

"All right," he said. Right before ending the call, he delivered his favorite line. "See you in court."

Blakely ended the call with an awkward thank-you.

"Everything all right at the hospital?" Dalton asked, breaking through the thoughts rolling around in her head.

"Yes," she said, refocusing on him. Her stomach gave a little flip the moment their gazes touched. "My law professor showed up with flowers."

Dalton's face twisted. "You two must be close."

"Not really," she said. "He sometimes brings students to observe a trial for extra credit and has introduced me to some of his contacts, but I don't know him beyond a professional level."

"Bringing flowers sounds kind of personal if you ask me," he said.

"He listens to scanners like an ambulance chaser to illustrate how they can be used to find clients," she said.

"Does he find clients that way?"

"He's a professor, so it's an academic exercise to him," she explained.

A clank in the hallway caused them both to freeze.

Dalton moved, breaking through the temporary hold first.

"Hide underneath your desk," Dalton said, already to his feet as Blakely reached for the key that unlocked the drawer with her Sig Sauer.

It dawned on her just how poetic it might be for someone like Johnny Spear to kill her in her chambers. It was, after all, this courthouse where his life was changed forever.

Drawer unlocked, fingers curled around the butt of the gun, she'd be ready for whatever walked through that door.

Chapter Twelve

Dalton had his weapon drawn before he exited Blakely's chambers. He slipped out to the small reception area and flattened his back against the wall. Slowly, purposefully, he made his way toward the door leading to the hallway.

Stopping next to the door, he listened. A list of folks who might be at the courthouse late on a Sunday ran through his mind. Maintenance. Custodial. Another judge. Security guard.

Yes, it dawned on him that word could have spread about the judge's attack. Law enforcement circles ran small, sometimes shockingly small. It was another reason a relationship wouldn't be a good idea, especially now that he'd been assigned to protect her.

Approaching thirty had him questioning how much he loved his job despite what he'd said to her at the hospital. A growing piece of him missed working the paint horse ranch alongside his family members. He was realizing how lonely it could be moving to a new city where he worked much of the time. He volunteered for extra duty in order to fill his days.

Now, he was starting to wonder why. He'd had an independent streak a mile long growing up. Was he getting softer as he got older?

The clank of keys on a key ring sounded on the opposite side of the door. Could be custodial. Or security.

His truck was registered to him personally. It had been the vehicle he'd been driving when the protection assignment had come in. Security might red-flag his truck if they'd driven by.

The business end of his gun aimed at the door, he held steady as he waited to see if the door handle moved or a key slid into the lock. There would be a second or two for him to identify himself as a marshal before a decision to shoot might have to be made. Dalton had been forced into a position of discharging his weapon on multiple occasions. He never took it lightly that one of his bullets could end a life. Criminal or not, everyone's right to live was respected by Dalton.

Several seconds passed without another sound on the other side of the door. It felt almost like a standoff. But did the person out there even suspect that someone could be on the other side of this door?

His logical side kicked in, reminding him there were a whole lot of reasons someone might stop. The first of which was to read and respond to a text. There were other reasons. Like the person could be cleaning.

Being in law enforcement had tainted him in many ways. It made him suspicious of everyone and everything. It made him sit in restaurants facing the door so no one could sneak up on him. And it made him snap to worst-case scenarios.

Silence stretched on for what felt like an eternity. Patience won during times like these. Lucky for him, his stubborn streak engaged.

And then he heard someone whistling. He dropped down to check the crack underneath the door. The small sliver offered enough of a view to lead him to believe someone from the custodial department was doing his job.

On a slow exhale, he pushed to standing and returned to Blakely once he was certain the man had moved down the hallway.

"False alarm?" she asked before setting a Sig Sauer on top of her desk. Even from here, seven feet away from her, he could see her hands trembling. Did she believe she could steady herself enough to hit a mark? A thump of adrenaline could cause her to shoot the wrong person. Or miss entirely.

"Looks like it," he said, keeping an ear toward the hallway. "Now that you have a name, do you think we should head out?"

"To go where?" she asked. "My home isn't safe any longer."

"We should have packed an overnight bag," he admitted.

"I have court in the morning," she said. Her stomach picked that moment to growl.

His place was a mess. Laundry was piled on the floor in his bedroom. His normal chores were put on hold once the call came in. Still, his apartment was safer than going home. "I have a spare bedroom. Can't promise much in the way of comfort, but—"

"No, thanks," she said, cutting him off.

"Do you have a better idea?" he asked, trying his level best to hide the fact his ego was bruised by the express rejection.

"I should probably stay at Bethany's house," she said. "I'd like to be there for Chase, especially in the morning before he's taken to school. It's been a hard weekend for him and…" It seemed to dawn on her that a murderer was stalking her. She shook her head. "That's a bad idea, isn't it?"

"Not completely," he reassured her. "Chase probably does need you."

"But I could be bringing a murderer to his doorstep," she said. "He could end up in the hospital like Bethany. If she hadn't been at my house and we weren't on the couch this morning, she—" The helpless look she shot him was quickly followed by her squaring her shoulders and lifting her chin up. "I know what you're going to say. I can't think like that. But wouldn't you if the situation was reversed?"

Dalton started to speak but bit his tongue instead. After giving reality a few seconds to kick in, he said, "My initial response is no, but that's just the US marshal talking. As a human being who loves his family and would do anything to protect them if they needed protecting, I would blame myself just like you're doing right now." He paused for a beat. "It still wouldn't be true, but I'd do the same."

She took in a deep breath and smiled.

"Do you know how to use that weapon?" he asked, motioning toward the Sig.

"I've been to the shooting range," she admitted. "Can't say that I'm an expert marksman, but I've taken a couple of classes."

"Where was it?"

Blakely motioned toward a drawer. "I keep it locked inside my desk. It's just for emergencies."

"Do you want to lock it up before we head out?" he asked. "I can take you anywhere you want to go."

A surprising helpless look crossed her features for a split second before she recovered. "I have no idea where that is." She threw her hands up.

"Since you don't want to go to my place, I could see if I can call in a favor or request a safe house," he offered.

"No, no," she repeated. "Your place is fine if the offer still stands."

"I can make a mean steak," he said.

"I remember."

"Does that sound good?" he asked. "We can pick up a couple of ribeye on the way home."

"Okay," she said, tension lines forming around her mouth—a mouth that had burned against his a little while ago. "If you don't mind cooking. Because we could pick up something to take back, or I can order something for delivery."

"I don't mind," he reassured her.

It was probably more of his bruised ego talking, but he didn't like the fact her law professor had tracked her to the hospital. He must have believed that he would find her lying in the bed instead of her sister. He understood keeping up professional connections in a small world. But showing up at the hospital made Dalton believe the professor might be interested in more.

Blakely wasn't naïve, but he also didn't think she realized how desirable she was or how interesting she was to talk to. Dalton didn't do long talks after sex, and yet he had with her. They might have kept professional details out of the picture, but they'd discussed everything from favorite foods to favorite colors.

He didn't do that either. He didn't get too personal with the women he spent time with. Dinner and a movie, their pick on both counts. Walks in the park. One of the women he'd dated had been more into fitness than him. But his abs had never looked better than when they were together because her favorite activity was working out at the park. He didn't argue. The workouts were intense. The sex was decent. But when he had to fight with the mirror for her attention, he'd drawn the line.

Then, there'd been the hairdresser who'd tried to convince him to shave the sides of his head and leave a thick patch on top. Not quite a mohawk or mullet. Definitely not him. He'd learned early on to walk away from anyone who saw him as someone they could change. She'd been into fashion and the latest trends while he'd been content to watch a game on his day off.

Lately, though, he was starting to feel like he was missing out on something. He blamed his family. All three of his cousins had found the loves of their lives. Until recently, he hadn't believed in such a thing. He and his brother, Camden, were the lone holdouts. Or, maybe the lone *missing outs*. He couldn't be certain which one.

Or had it been his time with Blakely that had changed his mind? Opened him to new possibilities?

"READY?" BLAKELY SAID after clearing her throat while she closed and then locked the gun drawer.

"Mind if I step into the hallway to make sure no one is out there?" Dalton asked.

"Go for it," she said as she closed her laptop and then rounded the desk. She'd bought the Sig never in a million years expecting to have to use it one day. It was meant to be insurance. And like most policies, no one ever intended to need to cash them in before they were good and ready.

She wasn't ready to shoot someone. Being around guns at all ushered her back to that chilly Sunday morning when Eric, her fifteen-year-old ex-boyfriend, had shown up at her home wild-eyed and blank-faced. Distant. Like he'd gone somewhere far away mentally, and no one could reach him again.

She remembered his anger the moment he'd jumped her and put the sharp blade to her throat. He'd held her head back and threatened to call her sister outside so Bethany could watch as he sliced Blakely from ear to ear.

Somehow—she could never remember the exact details—she'd managed to drop down and avoid having her throat sliced. Her forehead was another matter. That had been cut while she'd fought Eric. He'd been strong. Stronger than she remembered.

"Hey," Dalton said to her, breaking through the memory and bringing her back to the present. "Are you all right?"

"To be honest, Dalton, I'm not real sure that I'll ever be all right again, but I'm going to do what I always do."

"What's that?" he asked.

"I'm going to keep on keeping on, no matter who tries to stop me or what bastard thinks they can take me out," she said, pulling on all her strength. After Eric, she'd promised herself that no one got to make her feel weak again. No one got to make her scared of her own shadow again. And no one got to take away her sense of safety and security again. "If Johnny Spear wants to come for me, he better be ready for a fight."

"Good," he said to her. "Because that's exactly the person I wanted to get to know more in Galveston that weekend. And since we'll be spending a lot of time together until this case is resolved, I hope to see more of that fight in you."

"Do you have any regrets?" she asked before adding, "Tell me honestly."

"About us?" he asked, cocking an eyebrow.

"Yes," she managed to say.

"I think it's unfortunate we met when we did," he said. "And if I could turn back time, I'd rewind the clock and do things a whole lot differently."

"That's probably good," she said, his words the equivalent of a knife through the center of her chest. Despite the heat in the kiss they'd shared, which to be fair, might have been more on her side than his, he seemed to have a lot of regret when it came to her. It was good. It might keep them from making another mistake—though, she couldn't bring herself to categorize that weekend as a bad thing. Time waited for no one. It moved on. And she needed to move on with it. They'd shared a moment in the past. Key words being *in the past*. Today was a new day, and she needed to get with the program no matter how strong the pull was to this man or how damn good he smelled when they were close. She'd memorized his woodsy and spicy all-male scent. Her fingers had mapped the lines and curves in his back.

"Do you think so?" he hedged.

"I believe everything turned out the way it should have," she quipped, masking the hurt she felt in his words. In order to keep herself safe, she had to keep everyone else at arm's length. Since Eric, she couldn't afford to let her guard down with anyone. Even her relationship with Bethany changed after that day. Bethany became needier, and Blakely stepped even more into a parenting role.

Did she have regrets?

The short answer was yes. But since she didn't dwell on the past or mistakes, she pulled herself up by her bootstraps and moved on.

Except when it came to Dalton. For some reason, a reason she didn't want to acknowledge or examine, she couldn't seem to move on. The recent kisses they'd shared were right up there with the best of her life. No one had ever even come close to making her want to stick around or dig deeper into someone's mind until Dalton.

Leaving him again was going to open those still-fresh wounds. Was there an alternative?

Chapter Thirteen

Dalton's apartment was messier than he remembered. Or maybe he was just more embarrassed at bringing Blakely home to any mess when her home had been neat as a pin. He mumbled an apology as he moved to the patio to fire up the grill.

"Do you mind fixing those inside so you won't be exposed?" Blakely asked as her gaze swept the twin building out the window and the parking lot in between.

"Okay," he conceded. He had one of those fancy stoves with a grill top. It wasn't as good as outdoor grilling, but she had a point. No matter how much of a long shot, someone might have figured out the two of them were together and identified him. It would take both of those for someone to get his address since he was certain no one had followed them from the courthouse. *Better safe than sorry.* His grandmother Lacey's voice had a habit of popping up in situations like these. Thinking about her was too hard, so he stuffed the memory down deep.

"I'll do the baked potatoes," Blakely offered. "It'll give my hands something to do."

"Fair enough," he said. "Let me know when you're about twenty minutes out." In the meantime, he could let the steaks rest after peppering them with Lawry's Seasoned Salt.

"Will do," she said as she preheated the oven.

Normally, a cold beer would sound good about now. But his mind needed to be clear. Being around Blakely was distraction enough. Every time he walked past her or needed to stand beside her, he breathed in her clean floral and citrus scent. Every time their skin grazed, electricity pulsed through him. Every time his gaze dropped to her lips, an ache formed deep in his chest.

Rather than torture himself by focusing on someone he could never have, he excused himself from the kitchen to straighten up.

Blakely's cell buzzed in the next room. She grabbed it from her handbag and then checked the screen. The look that crossed her features before she dropped the phone into her purse again brought on questions. "Everything okay?"

"Yes," she said without turning to face him. Was she hiding her expression or was he reading too much into the situation?

Dalton finished straightening up by tossing clean and dirty clothes into a laundry basket that he set on top of the washer in the hallway between the two bedrooms.

"Did you just move in?" Blakely asked as he joined her in the kitchen.

"I just signed a lease for another year," he said.

"Oh," she said as her cheeks flushed with embarrassment.

"What gave you that impression?" he asked, doing his level best to keep a straight face. It was obvious to anyone who walked in, but he wanted to hear her version.

"I didn't mean to make an assumption," she said. Was she trying to spare his feelings? "But there's not one picture hanging on the walls, so I just assumed."

"Did anything else tip you off?" he asked, continuing with the blank-face routine to see how far he could push it.

"The packing box sitting next to the front door," she said, looking like she was choosing her words carefully.

Dalton broke into a wide smile. "This is my second year living here, but I haven't made the time to finish unpacking." He chuckled as she made a face at him. "What? I wanted to give you enough rope to hang yourself because you seemed so worried that I might get offended."

"Thanks for the save," she quipped, but then she laughed too. And then they both laughed in a manner that far outweighed the joke.

Blakely pinched her side but couldn't stop. "I really thought you might be doing your best here."

Dalton couldn't hold a serious face if he tried. "I might not have your decorating skills, but I do realize when a house hasn't been unpacked yet. I've got eyes."

"Really? Because for a minute, I thought you couldn't see that walls need pictures or art, or something on them so they don't look like dry-erase boards." More laughter broke out. It was good to see Blakely with a smile on her face for a change. The situation wasn't all that funny, but both needed a break in tension. Stress usually found an outlet in the form of tears or laughter. This time, Blakely was laughing so hard she cried, and he wasn't far behind.

When the laughter finally died down, Blakely said, "Why isn't there anything on the walls? Too busy?"

He shrugged. "The truth is that this place is a convenient location, but I can't say that it's ever felt like home."

"Why's that?" she asked. He resisted the urge to ask if she was sure about asking anything deemed too personal.

"I grew up on a ranch, so the land probably has something to do with it," he said. "I'm not sure what else the problem is, other than to say it doesn't feel like home."

"The building is tall and modern," she pointed out after careful thought. "What floor is this?"

"Seventeenth," he supplied.

"It strikes me as odd that you'd live so high in the air when you've always been a feet-on-the-ground person," she stated. The comment resonated. There was real insight in those words.

Dalton resisted the notion she might know him better than he knew himself. They'd spent a long weekend together before now, which wasn't nearly long enough to get to know a person. "Well, you have a point there, Your Honor."

It also dawned on him that she was most likely good at reading people and body language given her chosen profession. He could say the same about himself. It still had him scratching his head how he'd misjudged the situation that had happened with the two of them talking for hours about nothing the first night they'd met and then spending the night together making love. But that was probably coming from the bruised ego she'd left behind after walking, no, running, away from him.

Dating a coworker wasn't professional. Having sex with a coworker definitely wasn't considered professional. Technically, however, they weren't coworkers. They worked in the same district and in the same type of business. Their paths could cross. That was an obvious reality given the circumstances. It scorched him that she didn't believe he could be professional enough to handle the situation should they come face-to-face.

Now that he'd been assigned to protect her, having a fling was off the table. When they'd made love, she hadn't known him from Adam.

"We're twenty minutes out," she announced, cutting into his reverie.

Dalton moved into the kitchen, trading places while Blakely took his seat at the small table built for two. Moving around each other in the kitchen felt like a dance they'd rehearsed their entire lives. There was nothing more natural. "Hold on." He moved to the opened box in the living room, dug around and extracted a picture of all the cousins together at the paint horse ranch. They were young and fresh-faced, all sitting on top of a small stretch of wood fence, all smiling like they'd just been told they could eat nothing but ice cream for dinner. His cousin Crystal had found the picture years ago, had duplicates made and then framed for each one of them to put up in their homes since they all lived apart in different areas of Texas. This way, no matter where they were, they would always have each other. Or, at least, that was what she'd said while presenting the gifts.

He set the picture on the fireplace mantel, in the center. "There. Is that better?"

Blakely smiled. "Yes, it is."

He couldn't agree more.

Blakely watched as Dalton worked his magic on the stovetop grill. "Do you mind if I ask what drew you to law enforcement and becoming a marshal?"

"I'll tell if you will," he said. "And you go first."

These topics had been off-limits before, but there was nothing stopping them from sharing details about their private lives now.

"I had a run-in with someone when I was fifteen years old," she explained. "It resulted in the scar on my forehead." She paused a beat, realizing it was easier to talk about than she feared it might be. Was that the Dalton effect? "After that, it took a really long time to trust people again."

"I'm sure that must have left a huge imprint on you mentally," he said. "Being fifteen is hard enough without having a traumatic event to knock you off-balance."

He didn't know the half of it.

"I'm sorry that happened to you," he said with the kind of compassion that made her almost believe everything would be all right again. "It must have left a lasting impression."

"It did," she admitted. "But then I got strong physically and mentally, and I promised myself that I would do everything in my power to protect others from a similar fate."

"What happened to the person who did this to you?"

"He got off with a slap on the wrist because his family had enough money for an expensive lawyer. One who played golf with the judge who presided over the case," she said, realizing she hadn't spoken those words out loud in…ever.

"Sonofabitch," he mumbled, and she couldn't agree more. "So you studied law and decided to become a judge to protect those who can't protect themselves."

"Yes," she said, also realizing the irony in the fact one of those bastards was currently threatening her life after being released on a technicality. At least they knew who they were looking for now. There was a BOLO out. She had to trust law enforcement to do their jobs.

"It's noble," he said. "And I'm still sorry the bastard walked away without punishment."

"He self-destructed within a couple of years," she said before turning the tables. "How about you? Why did you become a US marshal?"

"Job security," he quipped. They both laughed at that. His job was one of the most dangerous paths in law enforcement.

"Seriously," she said.

"Okay," he said before flipping the steaks. They sizzled on the grill, and the place already smelled like heaven. "Here goes. I had a no-good mother who abandoned the family not long after I was born."

"Oh," she said. "That's awful."

"Thankfully, I was too young to remember that," he said. "Except that my father then died young. He was a good person by all accounts."

The phrase *only the good die young* came to mind. Though, experience had taught her that wasn't always the case.

"So my siblings and I were brought up by extremely loving grandparents on their paint horse ranch," he continued as though that explained everything. When she arched an eyebrow, he continued, "My grandfather was a US marshal. He is the most stand-up person I've ever met." He shrugged. "That was how he saved the money to buy the paint horse ranch for my grandmother. They eventually built the business enough for him to work the ranch full-time. I guess I figured if I could be anybody, I'd want to model my life after his."

Blakely had heard everyone who worked in law enforcement had a story. "Thanks for telling me yours."

"I never talk about my family," he admitted as the steaks sizzled. "They're done."

"I'll grab plates," she offered.

Dalton motioned toward a cabinet as he pulled the steaks off the heat. Standing next to him felt like the most natural thing.

"Here you go," she said to him as she held out a plate. He tossed a gorgeous ribeye on top with a smile that could cut through ice. "I wasn't so sure I'd be able to eat with everything going on. My stomach usually rebels first when I'm under stress. But my mouth is already watering."

"It's good to eat so you can keep up your strength," he said.

"After we eat, I'll make a call to the hospital to check on Bethany," she said.

"While you do that, I should check on my grandparents. They're in the hospital," he said.

"I'm hoping that no news is good news for both of us."

"Couldn't agree more," he said as he plated the second steak. They fixed up baked potatoes standing side by side. His spicy male scent filled her when she took in a deep breath. It would be so easy to lean into Dalton's strength. But then what? What would she do if she learned to depend on someone else?

Not everyone will let you down. Those words coming out of nowhere shocked the hell out of her. Were they true?

"This food is amazing," she said, redirecting her focus after sitting down and taking the first bite.

"Steak is my specialty," he said.

"Do you mind if I ask you another question?"

"Shoot," he said, before adding, "Forgive the word choice."

"Have you ever thought about reaching out to your mother?"

"No," he said in a tone that said *case closed*.

The question was a mood killer. The rest of the meal was spent in silence. When Blakely had taken the last bite, she said, "I'll clear the table and do the dishes."

"I can help," he said. She knew better than to argue when anyone offered help in the kitchen.

They each took their dishes to the sink. Not a bite was left on either, so they didn't need the trash disposal. After rinsing plates, knives and forks, she placed them in the dishwasher while he put on a pot of coffee.

"Do you want a cup?" he asked.

"It's too late for me," she said. "All I want is to know that my sister is still in stable condition, a shower and a bed."

"Take the main bedroom," he said, again in the tone that said arguing would be a mistake.

"Do you have anything I can change into for sleeping?"

"I'll put something out while you make the call to the hospital." With that, he disappeared down the hallway.

Blakely made the call. It was quick and to the point. Bethany was stable. No one else had come to see her.

Dalton returned a few moments later. "Lay your clothes out, and I'll throw them in the wash. We can get up early tomorrow to swing by your house before court."

Cooking in the kitchen and making plans to go back to work tomorrow were reassuring. It was the little things, she'd learned, that gave a sense of normalcy in difficult times.

"Okay," she said.

"I put a robe out for you to use," he said. "And an oversize T-shirt."

She liked the sounds of those things. After thanking him, she headed into his bedroom. It looked similar to the other rooms, unfinished. The bed was big and had comfortable-looking blankets and pillows. She tested it as she walked past. This was going to be like sleeping on a cloud.

A pink robe that was her size hung on the door to the bathroom. A sting of jealousy caught her off guard. She'd been clear there was no future for the two of them. Dalton was honest and respectable. He was honorable, which seemed in rare supply with people these days. All she had to do was take one look at her brother-in-law.

That wasn't completely fair. She didn't know the real ins and outs of her sister's marriage. Greg, no matter how off he seemed or how desperate he looked, was a decent person. He was clearly torn up about the affair he'd been having. He seemed...she didn't know the right word...maybe lost?

Seeing him at the hospital had been a wake-up call too. Bethany had been keeping secrets. She hadn't been confiding in Blakely. Guilt nearly consumed her at letting her younger sister down. If Blakely had known about the problems, she would have been able to help. It was possible the situation wouldn't have gone this far.

A shower helped wash the day away. Reluctantly, she wrapped herself in the pink robe after drying off. A toothbrush still in its wrapper waited on the counter. She brushed and then set her clothes outside the bedroom door for them to be washed.

When she opened the door, she heard the low hum of Dalton's voice. It reverberated through her, lighting all kinds of fires that didn't need to be lit. Was he talking to the owner of this pink robe? As much as she knew in her heart he wouldn't betray another woman by kissing her, they hadn't exactly talked about whether or not he was seeing someone.

Was it her business?

No.

Did a growing part of her *want* it to be her business?

Yes.

So, what did she plan to do about it?

the laundry basket. He threw on a pair of boxers and cotton workout shorts, grabbed a blanket after washing her clothes, and then rested his eyes while lying down on the sofa.

He rarely needed more than a cat nap when he was on a protection assignment, so he got up before the sun and finished the small load of laundry. The least he could do was give her clean clothes to wake up to. Handling her pink silk panties had sent blood flowing south, but he was no longer a hormonal teenager. He was a grown man, who was capable of doing laundry without needing a cold shower afterward.

Remembering how silky Blakely's skin had felt under his touch was another story. It created a visceral memory that was more difficult to tamp down.

Dalton almost laughed out loud. Grown man, huh?

A fresh cup of coffee helped wake him up. He was still full from last night, so he grabbed his phone and checked to see if a message had come through on the group chat. When he'd talked to Jules last night, she'd sounded hopeful there was a chance their grandfather would wake up again.

Of course, they'd been going down this road long enough for him to be educated on the fact someone in a coma could wake up, seem totally fine and then go right back under, never to wake again.

Too many weeks had passed for Dalton to expect this situation to end well. Duke, his cousin, mentioned that they might want to think about what they wanted to do with the ranch if their grandparents didn't make a meaningful recovery.

Dalton just wasn't there yet. He couldn't see a world where his strong-as-an-ox grandfather wasn't at the helm of Remington Paint Ranch.

This wasn't the time to think about comfort food, but he couldn't stop himself from wanting a chicken-fried steak from Mama Bea's place in Mesa Point. Every time he thought about the ranch, Mama Bea came up. Her food was the definition of heaven. A little voice in the back of his mind picked that moment to point out that he'd found heaven in everything when he was with Blakely.

He reminded himself how fast she'd bolted before and how little use there was in thinking there was even a remote possibility she would let him in her life, no matter how much electricity charged the air in between them every time they were within arm's reach of one another. Or how much his mouth ached to claim hers, marking her as his, when their gazes met. Or how sexy she was in a jogging suit. Of course, she was even sexier with nothing on.

"Good morning," she said after clearing her throat. He hadn't heard her open the bedroom door. She caught him off guard, especially considering he'd just pictured her naked. She held out the pink robe, which was folded up. "This belongs to you. Or should I say your girlfriend?"

"No girlfriend," he said quickly and with a little heat as he met her across the room. "Is that how little you think of me?"

"I wasn't sure what to think when you left out a pink ladies' bathrobe for me, Dalton."

Was she jealous?

"The robe belongs to my sister," he said. "She slept over on her way to serve a warrant, got a tip her felon was about to move and hightailed it out of here so fast she forgot to take her favorite robe with her." He crossed his arms over his chest. "It looked to be about your size, so I thought you might want to use it once you got out of the shower. But I didn't realize—"

"Never mind," she quipped, handing over the bundle. "I just thought something else. That's all. No big deal."

Well, it sure as hell sounded like a big deal to him. Or was that wishful thinking on his part?

"For the record, if you were in a relationship with someone else, it would be a very big deal to me," he said before walking out of the living room to set the robe on top of the washing machine.

When he returned to the kitchen, the sun had begun to rise, and Blakely nursed a cup of coffee while standing in his kitchen looking better than she had a right to.

"Hungry?" he asked.

"Not really," she said. She seemed content to let his comment fly past without acknowledgment. "We should probably head to my house so I can grab clothes for work." She issued a sigh. "Though, nothing in me wants to go back there."

"We can always stop by a twenty-four-hour big-box store instead," he said.

"No," she said. "I need to face it even if I don't want to."

"There's nothing wrong with giving yourself a minute, Blakely. You don't always have to make the hard decision and push through if you need a little more time."

She blew out a breath. "I've been pushing through life ever since I can remember. It got me through the deaths of my parents. It got me through the responsibility of taking care of my sibling. And it got me through both undergrad and law school. I'm one of the youngest judges seated in Texas. What if I don't know how to take more time? What if this is just who I am?"

Dalton was beginning to realize how much the story you told yourself about your life shaped it. "I think you're amazing, and you can be anything you want to be."

"What if I can't do it?"

"It might be hard, but if you put your mind to it, I doubt

there's anything you can't accomplish," he said and meant every word.

"Do you mean that, Dalton?"

"I've never been more certain of anything in my life," he reassured. "Plus, I've been told that I have a stubborn streak a mile long. Until I met you, I thought that was as far as a stubborn streak could go. You proved me wrong on that."

Blakely broke into a smile. "How is it that you can make me laugh so easily?"

"That's easy?" he shot back, matching her smile.

"Okay, tough guy," she said. "You better go get dressed while I come up with a plan to get in and out of my house without incident."

"I'll call to let my contact at Houston PD know we'll be heading that way so he can get eyes on the place," Dalton said before excusing himself and heading into the bedroom to grab clothes.

He dressed in a suit since he was taking Blakely to her courtroom. Once inside, it would be difficult if not impossible for Johnny Spear to get to her. On the way in was another story altogether, but he could alert the bailiff when they got close so extra eyes could be on her when Dalton dropped her off at the front door.

Leaving his apartment caused a bad feeling to settle in the pit of his stomach. Was he being overly cautious with Blakely due to their past?

Or their present?

WHOA! BLAKELY COULDN'T remember the last time she witnessed a man wearing a suit in the same way Dalton wore a suit. He filled out every thread of material that looked handspun by angels. What could she say? The man was perfection.

"You dress up nicely, Mr. Remington," she managed to say through a dry-as-desert throat. Was it suddenly getting hot in the apartment?

"Thank you, ma'am," he responded with a smile that could charm the pants off anyone with eyes. "After you." That same smile had been good at seducing her in Galveston. She'd been drawn to him like the magnet to steel cliché. The sister trip was supposed to be a chance for her and Bethany to catch up on each other's lives, spend some real time together. Except that Chase had gotten sick at the last minute, so Bethany had been needed at home. Since Blakely had funded the whole weekend and couldn't get her money back, she'd said *what the hell* and gone by herself on a whim.

Okay, she'd been feeling sorry for herself. She could admit that now. She'd realized how needed her sister was and how much the opposite was true for Blakely. No one would even notice if she disappeared off the face of the earth. That wasn't completely true. Bethany and Chase would miss her dearly. But they had each other, and they would be fine.

Sitting alone at the restaurant where she'd originally made a reservation for two had been beyond sad. Then, Dalton had walked in. He'd asked for a table for one and been told they couldn't seat him until after nine o'clock. He'd asked about placing a to-go order and had been told that could be arranged.

Without thinking, or in her case overthinking her next move, she'd waved him over and told him that she wouldn't mind the company if he wanted to eat with her. Eating at home alone every night was one thing. She was used to it. All she had to do was turn on the TV for background noise, and she was just fine. But eating out in public alone had just felt sad to her. The pity party she was having for herself had made her mad enough to ask a stranger to sit down. Dalton had thanked her and then told the hostess that he wasn't going to need to place a to-go order after all.

They'd made an agreement not to discuss work or anything too personal. But the night flew by. She couldn't even remember what either of them had said, but she remembered thinking, *This man is far too beautiful to be sitting here with me.*

The only information she'd divulged on a personal level was that she'd spent too many years in school but that she liked her job, so the long semesters spent with her nose in a book had turned out to be worth it after all.

He'd asked what her field of study had been. She'd laughed.

He'd asked if he could guess. She'd laughed.

He'd asked if he could walk her back to her hotel. She'd smiled and decided to take a chance.

After all, what was the harm in being escorted back to her hotel, considering she could see it from the restaurant? They'd sat in the lobby for another hour before she'd done something she never had before…invited him upstairs.

The next morning, he invited her to breakfast at the house he'd rented. "Were you on a stakeout when we met?" she asked him as the elevator dinged, indicating they were on the ground floor.

"No," he responded. "That would have been unprofessional."

She stepped out of the elevator and followed him through the first-floor lobby and to his truck. "Then what were you doing in Galveston?"

"It was work related," he said as he opened the door for her. She climbed in the passenger side and lowered the seat back to hide her face from view as much as possible. Dalton smiled approval at the move, and it gave her stomach a little flip.

He rounded the front of the truck and then reclaimed the driver's seat. "I was waiting for a felon to show up. We had good intel that he would be there any day, so we spread out and set up shop."

"How many of you were there?"

"From the Marshals office? Just me," he said. "But there was a task force on this one because he was on the most wanted list."

Blakely had been eating in a restaurant possibly with one of the worst criminals in America, and the man could have walked right past her and she wouldn't have known it. "Whoa. I'm guessing he never showed."

"You guessed correctly," he said. "In fact, he ended up on one of the cruise ships as staff two weeks later."

"So you wasted your time," she pointed out.

"Spending the weekend with you could never be considered a waste of time as far as I'm concerned," he said so low that she almost didn't hear him. Those words, though, sent more of that warmth circling through her, settling inside her thighs. Her body remembered his touch, craved it even now.

Where was logic when it came to matters of the heart?

Blakely cleared her throat. She couldn't think about how much she'd missed his touch in the weeks since. She couldn't think about how many times she'd had to force this man from her thoughts, especially at night when she tried to sleep but images of him kept popping into her mind. And she couldn't think about how right she'd felt in this man's arms and how safe, even if it only lasted a short time.

Blakely couldn't afford to give someone her safety. Besides, she'd gotten by fine on her own all these years. And she'd be fine moving forward.

So why did it feel like such a lie this time?

Chapter Fifteen

"Did you call the security company that patrols your neighborhood to let them know you'd be by this morning?" Dalton asked his now-quiet passenger. She'd been silent for longer than he was comfortable with. What was going on in that brilliant mind of hers?

"I should do that," she said, reaching for her cell. "I have a number that I can text so everyone will get the message. I'll let them know that we're on our way."

A few seconds later, she dropped her phone inside her purse again before leaning her head back.

"Did you sleep okay?" he asked.

"Sure," she said. "In fact, once I was out, I didn't open my eyes again until this morning. How about you?"

"I got in a couple hours of shut-eye," he said. "I don't need much." He hoped the small talk could keep her mind off returning to her house. Her body language had tensed once the subject came up. Talking had always calmed his sister and cousins when they had to face a scary task. He hoped the distraction would work for Blakely too.

"I'm normally an eight-hour girl," she said. "You don't want to talk to me before I've had my coffee either."

"Good to know," he said, remembering she'd had her coffee in hand when he joined her in the kitchen. "What about breakfast? Should we run through a drive-through?"

"I can grab a couple of protein bars at my house," she offered.

He got it. She didn't want to risk being stuck in a line if Johnny Spear caught up to them. Innocent people could get hurt, not to mention both of them shot. "Sounds like a plan." His coffee had kicked in, clearing the cobwebs. Though, he had the ability to snap into action on fifteen minutes of sleep and no caffeine if needed. His sister teased him about it being his superpower.

The situation with his grandparents got him thinking about family a whole lot. And about whether he wanted to stay on the job or not.

"Did you ever want to be anything else besides a judge?" he asked Blakely.

"Not really," she said. "Not seriously or when I was old enough to know the variety of jobs out there. I went through the usual I-want-to-be-a-veterinarian stage that most animal lovers go through when they're young. What about you?"

"I've been thinking about that question since the accident," he admitted. Dalton hadn't spoken to anyone about a pull toward changing professions. Not even his family. "I loved the parts of my childhood that allowed me to run free on the land. The ranch is a special place."

"Have you spoken to the others about what it might look like if your grandparents have a long recovery?" she asked. He appreciated the fact she hadn't said "when they die." He couldn't bring himself to believe they wouldn't pull through this, even though time was running out and they weren't making meaningful progress.

"No," he said. "But I've been thinking that conversation is probably overdue. After this assignment, it's my turn and then my brother Camden's. I'm not sure how long we can keep rotating like this. Plus, decisions are going to have to be made about the horses. It keeps the person who is holding vigil at the hospital busy since much of the work can be done via laptop until it's time to arrange a pickup."

"Growing up on a horse ranch sounds like the coolest childhood ever," Blakely said with appreciation in her voice.

"It's not for everyone, but it was special to me," he admitted.

"Would you consider going back and taking over for your grandparents full-time?" she asked.

"It was never even a thought until recently," he said as he entered her neighborhood. "Now? I guess I'm considering all options."

"Would you regret leaving your job?"

"How will I know if I don't try it?" he asked before turning the tables. "Would you ever consider doing anything else for a living?"

"Never say never," Blakely said. "But, I've been so busy making my mark that I haven't taken the time to consider any other path. I'm proud of the work that I've done and how far I've come." She shrugged as they pulled up in front of her home where a squad car waited. "And I know that I don't want to be on the other side of the bench as a litigator. So what else would I do?"

"I don't know," he said. "Maybe work as a victim's advocate. I could see you doing something like that." His tactic to keep her talking worked. She'd relaxed enough to stop working her fingers into a knot. That was progress.

"Guess I never thought about it," she said. "Once I decided on law, I gave myself no other options because that was the only way to succeed in getting through law school."

A uniformed officer exited his vehicle to walk to the truck, as Dalton did the same before rounding the front to open Blakely's door.

He surveyed the area and then tucked Blakely behind him.

After perfunctory greetings, the officer followed closely behind as they essentially formed a shield around Blakely.

She was in and out of the house in less than ten minutes. It had to be some kind of record for getting ready, and she shouldn't look this good without making much effort. Though, Dalton wouldn't complain.

Thick hair in a slicked-back ponytail, she looked every bit the serious judge. Except Dalton had never seen a judge as beautiful.

They made it to the truck without incident, thanked the officer and then doubled back toward the courthouse.

Once settled and out of her neighborhood, Blakely pulled a couple of power bars out of her handbag, as promised, and handed one over.

Dalton polished his off in a matter of four bites. Blakely ate hers slowly, staring out the window as she chewed on every bite.

"You might be right about becoming a victim's advocate," she said once she'd finished hers. Next, she pulled out a pair of bottled waters. "Thirsty?"

"What else do you have in there? A breakfast taco?" he teased.

Blakely's serious expression broke, and she smiled. "I threw everything in here but the kitchen sink."

"Oh, darn," he teased. "How will I wash my hands without a sink?"

Blakely exhaled. "Thank you, by the way."

He shot a confused look her way.

"First of all, you didn't ask to be reassigned the minute you realized who you'd be protecting on this assignment," she began. "I might not have acted like it at first, but I'm glad it's you and not some stranger."

"You're welcome." He probably shouldn't be thanked for doing his job. Though, he appreciated the gesture.

"Secondly, you haven't run off after everything," she said. "I should have explained myself. I should have figured out your number and called or told you what I did for a living instead of taking off without an explanation."

"About that," he said, surprised she'd brought it up. "What happened there? Did you think I was such a jerk that I wouldn't understand?"

"No, not that at all," she quickly countered. "I panicked. Plain and simple. I have no excuse for my actions, and I'm sorry."

"Apology accepted," he reassured her.

"And then I kissed you yesterday, which I had no place doing," she continued.

"No, and it can't happen again." They'd been doomed from the beginning. She realized that before he did. And he'd nursed a bruised ego, but he'd moved past it all and had no intention of going down that road.

"I know."

Why the hell did those words inch their way through the wall he'd constructed when it came to Blakely?

BLAKELY HAD NO idea why she felt the need to explain her actions, except that Dalton deserved to know the truth. "It's just that I'm broken, and I'm no good for anyone for the long haul. You know what I mean?"

Before he could respond, she added, "That fifteen-year-old who put this scar here was my boyfriend. I thought I loved him. And, yes, I know that what I felt was puppy love, first crush, but you know, it sure felt like the real thing to me then."

"First love is powerful," he said, taking it all in without

a hint of judgment in his expression. She loved that about him. He seemed to see the good in her.

"I haven't... I don't... I just don't think relationships are right for everyone," she said. "Take me, for instance. I'm completely happy alone. I have my sister and I have Chase." If this divorce happened like she feared it might, she would be seeing a whole lot more of Bethany and Chase. As it was, Blakely wanted to bring her sister home from the hospital to live with her until she sorted out her marriage. "They are going to need me more than ever."

Dalton nodded, but his grip tightened on the steering wheel.

"And I need to be there for them," she said. "Plus, my job is my life, and I spend the rest of my waking hours reviewing cases."

"You take care of everyone around you," he said in an unreadable tone.

"It's what I've always done," she said. Being the oldest, even by a few minutes, she'd stepped in to be there for Bethany after they lost their parents, and she intended to be there for her sister now.

"One question," Dalton said.

"Okay," she said.

"Who takes care of you?"

The question was simple. So why did it kick up a dust storm of emotions that caused hot tears to well in her eyes? "I do." Her voice cracked.

"As far as I can tell, you take care of everyone around you," he said, his voice wrapping around her like a warm embrace. It threatened to shatter all the carefully constructed walls she'd built around her heart.

Could she afford to let someone in?

Heart racing faster than if she'd just sprinted across the

parking lot, she wished she could. It was too much, too soon, too unknown.

"I think I've been doing a decent job of managing my life," she said.

"I didn't mean to—"

"What? Imply that I wasn't? Because what other logic is there for making a comment like that one?" Damn. She could hear the defensiveness in her own tone. "You're saying that I'm not competent to take care of myself. And that I'm incapable of managing my life."

"Hold on a second," Dalton said, still calm as the surface of a lake on a clear day. "You got all that from what I said?"

"It's what you meant, isn't it?"

"No, seriously. You extrapolated a criticism of your professional life as well as your personal life based on what I said?" He white-knuckled the steering wheel.

When he put it in those words, she sounded off base. It had made sense in her head a few seconds ago. "Sorry, would you repeat your statement?"

"Why? You're just going to decide what I mean instead of hearing me out anyway," he said. The finality in his tone said they were done talking about this.

Had she jumped to conclusions?

Maybe. Okay, yes. Yes, she'd jumped to conclusions, but that didn't mean she was off base.

"It's all I know," she said quietly as she stared out the front windshield.

"My grandmother used to say, 'If it's not broke, don't fix it.' Sounds like the saying applies here."

Blakely doubted she could change if she wanted to. "I'm set in my ways, Dalton."

"Okay," he said. His quick agreement struck like a physical blow. "We're here." He pulled up to the front doors of the courthouse, as close as possible. Ralph, her favorite bailiff, waited at the door. "You should probably head on inside."

A moment of panic gripped her. "Where will you be?"

"I'll be around," he said.

Okay. She'd done it. She'd successfully pushed him away. She'd done this, without regret, to every person who came into her life for longer than she cared to remember.

Why did she suddenly feel hollow inside?

Blakely was midtrial on a robbery case. She expected closing arguments later today, and then the jury would go into the jury room and start their process.

As she passed by the men's bathroom on the way to her courtroom, her law professor stepped into the hallway. The move caught her off guard. She yelped and brought a defensive hand up to push him away.

"Your Honor," he began, tipping his hat and offering a slight bow.

Before he could continue, she asked, "Professor, what are you doing here?"

"I brought a couple of promising students to witness a trial," he explained. The professor had a full head of white hair. He was tall, roughly six feet, and in his midfifties.

"Extra credit?" she asked, unable to muster a smile.

"That's right," he said, standing a little too close. "I'd hoped to catch you." His gaze shifted from her to Ralph and back. "Might I have a word in private?"

"Is it urgent?" she asked as an icky feeling took hold. "Because I'm on my way to court."

"Of course." His smile was more like a sneer. "It can wait."

Blakely tried to shake off the grimy feeling on her way to the bench.

"Everything all right, Your Honor?" Ralph asked.

"Fine," she said, even though she felt anything but.

Chapter Sixteen

Dalton surveyed the area for a long moment after Blakely disappeared inside the building. There was no sign of trouble. None that he could see anyway, which didn't necessarily mean a threat wasn't there.

Once Blakely was safely inside, he parked and then walked the perimeter. The parking lot itself wasn't busy. Half the spaces were empty. Jurors were most likely already present. This new-construction building had a dozen courtrooms. Summoned jurors were being sorted through in a large room, given assignments. Others had cases underway and were already seated in court.

Badge visible on his belt clip, he walked corridors and poked his head in rooms to get a baseline. So far, so good.

He'd seen Johnny Spear's picture, so he knew what facial features to look for. There were countless ways to alter your appearance, but Dalton was skilled at sifting through hair color changes and the various other ways to conceal your real identity. Clothing was another big one. Throw on a dress, put on makeup and paint your nails, and someone like Johnny could walk around freely without being identified.

The probability that Johnny could breach the courthouse might be slim, considering all the ID checks and fail-safes implemented, but Dalton left nothing to chance.

When he'd dotted every *i* and crossed every *t*, he located

Blakely's courtroom and found a seat in the back row. There was a small sprinkling of attendees. A gentleman with white hair sitting by three college-aged kids gave rapt attention not to the defendant or the litigators, but to Blakely.

Was this the law professor who'd shown up at the hospital? Didn't that make the tiny hairs on the back of Dalton's neck prickle? The man seemed to be stalking Blakely. This felt like more than just following her career. Dalton needed to have a conversation with her to get her take on the situation. This whole bit rubbed him the wrong way. Not once had any of his college professors tried to establish a personal connection outside of the classroom.

To be fair, she was remarkable and very successful at a young age. He was certain her university would want to keep a strong alumni connection.

Dalton's cell buzzed in his pocket. After checking the screen, he slipped out of the courtroom. "Hey, Jules. What's up?"

"It's Grandpa Lor," she began, emotion making the words come out strained.

"Everything okay?" His pulse spiked.

"He's awake," she managed to say clearly. "And he's asking for everyone."

"I'm on my way," Dalton replied before ending the call. His next was to his supervisor. "I need to go. Now. My grandfather's condition has improved."

"That's good news," Jamison Fox said. Most called him Foxy behind his back. The females on staff said he could pull off the name given his good looks. He wore a gold bracelet around his wrist with his wife and two young kids' names inscribed on it. His devotion to family, they'd said, made him *People*'s Sexiest Man Alive eligible in their books. "I'm happy for you, Dalton."

"I'm mid-assignment," Dalton began.

"Not a problem," Foxy said. "I'll pull someone and send them over. Where are you?"

"In court," Dalton said before explaining Blakely was well protected while in the courthouse.

"Go be with your family, Dalton."

He hesitated before thanking his supervisor. The thought of leaving Blakely sat hard on his chest. Harder than he expected. *A break would be good*, the little voice in the back of his mind reminded. They'd hit a wall on the personal front. Being with Blakely twenty-four-seven wasn't doing good things to his heart or his mind. A little time apart might help clear his head because their attraction was becoming a problem. For him, at least. She'd been clear about where she stood on having anything but a professional relationship.

"I'll have someone over before the end of the day," Foxy said. "Don't worry. I've got this. We'll protect the judge."

The reassurance helped, easing some of the guilt he felt for abandoning her.

"I appreciate it," Dalton said.

"Mesa Point is a couple hours' drive," Foxy said. "You should get on the road if you want to be there by lunch."

"Will do, boss," Dalton said, then thanked his supervisor once again before ending the call. He was torn right down the middle. Half of him wanted to give Blakely a heads-up before he took off. The other half reminded him that she'd been clear about taking care of herself. She'd been clear about not needing anyone in her life.

Walking away while his pride was still somewhat intact was his best bet. If it hurt now, imagine what it would feel like if he spent more time around her.

Closure. This was closure. So why did he feel like he had a big, gaping open wound where his heart should be?

OUT OF THE corner of her eye, Blakely saw Dalton slip out of the courtroom. Hours passed, and he didn't return. Had something happened? Had Dalton been called out? Was something happening in the building or parking lot?

Or had Johnny Spear been caught? Case closed?

At noon, she ordered a break for lunch. Ralph escorted her to her chambers, where she half expected Dalton to be waiting. Her heart sank to her toes when she found the space empty instead.

Still no sign of Dalton when it was time to head back into the courtroom. On the way, she leaned into Ralph and asked, "Have you seen my US marshal escort anywhere?"

"No, Your Honor," Ralph replied as he walked her back to the bench.

Was this bad news? Had something gone down?

"Have you heard any commotion?" she asked.

"No, I haven't," he responded before taking his post.

For the rest of the afternoon, there was no sign of Dalton. The trial concluded, and the jury convened to discuss a verdict. Once again, she waited alone in her chambers until the straightforward case was about to conclude. The jury was out for no longer than fifteen minutes before the announcement came that they were ready to deliver their verdict.

Still no sign of Dalton, and the day was almost over.

Would he be waiting in the truck?

At least the professor and his students were gone when court resumed. Blakely went through her usual bit before asking the jury foreman to read the verdict.

"Your Honor, we, the jury, find the defendant, Thomas Dunn, guilty of armed robbery," the foreman said, reading from a piece of paper.

"Thank you," Blakely said as the door to the courtroom opened and a man in a suit slipped in. He had that law-enforcement swagger she'd learned was as much part of the job as a neat haircut. This man had military-short red hair.

Her stomach dropped because there was still no sign of Dalton.

She delivered the maximum sentence to the defendant and then dismissed everyone before returning to her chambers. Red immediately knocked at the door as she reached for her purse, ready to get out of there and back to Dalton's apartment.

"My name is Lenn Gunnard," Red said. "I'm here as a replacement for Dalton Remington."

"Oh," she said, trying not to sound panicked despite her pulse spiking. "Is everything okay with Marshal Remington?" Did he despise her enough after their last discussion to ask to be removed from the case?

"Yes, Your Honor," Lenn supplied. "Family emergency."

Was that an excuse or did something happen with his grandparents? "I understand. I hope everyone is okay." Suddenly, she couldn't find a better word to use than *okay*. Where did her extensive vocabulary go? The one she'd used at mock trial during law school that had impressed her professors so much?

"I'm not certain," the marshal said. "I have a truck in the parking lot. Ralph said he would wait out front until I texted it was safe to come outside."

"Okay," she said. There was that word again. "Thank you."

Lenn disappeared as Ralph stepped into view.

"Ready, Your Honor?" Ralph asked.

"Yes," she said even though her thoughts were with Dalton and his family. What if something bad happened? Could she reach out to him? Would he even take her call?

Probably not.

But he couldn't stop her from showing up.

"I have an idea, Ralph," she said. "Would you be willing to give me a ride home?"

"Yes, Your Honor," he said.

"Any chance we can slip out the back?" she asked.

Ralph stood there for a moment before answering. "We can do that."

"I'd owe you big-time," she said.

"No, you wouldn't," he said with a wink. She could guess what it meant, but she wasn't ready to go there and admit to having feelings for Dalton with anyone. If she thought their relationship had a snowball's chance in hell of surviving the long haul, Dalton would be the first to know. She just didn't want to explain that she needed to get to the hospital in Mesa Point, Texas, to a stranger. Whether he liked it or not, she wanted to be there for Dalton in case the worst had just happened. He deserved that much from her, especially because she couldn't give him anything else, even if she wanted to. And a growing part of her wanted to.

"Then, let's go," she said after grabbing her handbag. They made their way out the back and to his truck without incident.

"I have a back way out of the parking lot that should keep us from driving past your new bodyguard," Ralph said. The spark in his voice said he was up for the adventure.

"I appreciate what you're doing," she said to him. "And I'll text the marshal so he isn't waiting all night. But I'd like to get a head start first because I'm sure he'll head straight to my home, where I need to go to pick up my car."

"What about the docket?" Ralph asked.

"I might be back by morning," she said, realizing she hadn't gotten past ditching the marshal out front. "But I'll call out once I get on the road with my car. And I'll take all the heat for asking you for a ride."

"Wasn't worried," Ralph said.

When they had a ten-minute head start, she texted the new marshal and said she would meet him back at the courthouse in an hour. Then half expected him to blow up her phone with messages. He sent one.

Don't worry about it. You'll be reassigned.

Did that mean Dalton was being put back on the case? Her heart double-crossed her, flipping, at the thought.

Calm down. She couldn't be certain of anything right now, and there was no use getting worked up if the man refused to ever set eyes on her again.

Her home wasn't far from the courthouse. Ralph walked her to her car as she dug out the keys.

"Be safe," he said once she was in the driver's seat.

"I will," she promised before closing and locking the door. She started the engine and backed out of the driveway as Ralph waved.

He became smaller and smaller in the rearview until he disappeared altogether. She'd made it into her subdivision. Now, she needed to make it to the highway. This time of year, it was already dark outside. Her stomach growled, making her wish she'd thought to throw a couple power bars inside her purse. She could stop once she got down the highway. Houston traffic was relentless.

Almost out of her subdivision, an aggressive vehicle pulled up from behind. The cab of the SUV was dark, the windows tinted. Bright headlights made it impossible to see who was behind the wheel. Her heart jackhammered the inside of her ribcage.

Was she going to have a reaction every time something felt off? Hadn't she stopped panicking over every little thing years ago?

The engine behind her gunned as she approached a four-way stop. The next thing she knew, her back bumper was being rammed. The SUV didn't have a front license plate, which was illegal in Texas. However, many vehicle owners ignored the regulation, and police didn't have time or resources to pull vehicles over for every minor infraction.

The SUV pushed her out into the intersection as a vehicle came rolling up. She mashed the gas pedal and hooked a last-minute right, staying in her neighborhood. She knew these roads like the back of her hand.

Whipping down an alley and then making another right, the SUV kept close enough to watch her every move. Blakely released a string of curses that would have made her mother blush.

And then she wheeled left, cutting down a back road. She maneuvered through the alley that would dump her onto an outside street. The highway wasn't far. She would have a better chance of losing the SUV on the highway.

In the meantime, she tried to use her voice to have her phone call for help. Of course, the phone didn't respond. She'd never had much luck with that thing.

Glancing in the rearview, she realized she was alone. Hot damn. She'd lost the SOB who'd been on her bumper. The close call jacked her pulse through the roof and scared her. Losing the marshal didn't seem like the best plan in hindsight.

But she'd done it. She'd lost the SUV and could maneuver out of the neighborhood and onto the highway. Once she could exhale, she would call and report the incident to

Chapter Fourteen

Dalton wouldn't be able to sleep if he tried. The update from his sister, Jules, had his stomach burning and his mind churning. His grandfather woke up for five minutes. Unfortunately, Jules had been outside grabbing a little sunshine to rejuvenate after what had been a long night of sleeping in fits and starts.

Essentially, when their grandparents needed someone to be in the room, no one had been there. He didn't blame Jules. She was one person and doing a helluva fine job being "on" nearly twenty-four hours a day. She needed support. Maybe it was a mistake to have only one person on duty. The job might be too much for one individual to cope with. And yet, he couldn't leave Blakely right now either. Did that make him the worst human in the world?

For someone who claimed to always put family first, how many holidays had he been home for in recent years? Not many. In fact, he volunteered to work so others could be home with their kiddos. Murderers didn't take holidays off. In fact, they had a habit of striking when opportunity presented itself.

A cold chill raced down his back at the thought of Johnny Spear getting to Blakely.

Dalton shook off the thought as best as he could, took a shower in the hall bath and then routed for clean clothes in the Houston PD. If Johnny Spear was close, she wanted the law to know.

Halfway through the next intersection, a vehicle sped up and T-boned her. Her sedan went into a spin as the SUV hit Reverse, backed up to make another run for her, miscalculated and got momentarily hung up on a fire hydrant.

Gunning the engine, she made her move, speeding through the neighborhood toward the highway as she frantically checked her rearview mirror, expecting the SUV to show up any second.

The incident rattled her to the point where her hands shook.

And then she caught a glimpse of him speeding toward her.

She smacked the steering wheel with the flat of her palm as she neared the on-ramp. Freedom was within arm's reach. *Come on. Come on. Go faster.*

Could she get there in time?

Chapter Seventeen

"I can't believe you're here," Jules said to Dalton as they stepped into the hallway to head to the waiting room, where a fresh pot of coffee waited.

"It's good to be home," he said. *Home.* Oddly, he'd had the same feeling when he was around Blakely. But it was no use. Her mind was made up. He had no idea what he was offering her anyway. And even if he had a clue, she'd been honest about needing to be alone.

After hearing the reason behind the scar on her forehead, he couldn't blame her for going into protect-herself-at-all-costs mode. As much as he wanted a chance to see where a relationship might go between them, it took two to tango. She was both unwilling and unable to meet him halfway.

As much as he hated to admit defeat, it was time to cash in his chips when it came to the sexy judge.

"Grandpa Lor is looking alert," Dalton said, switching topics in an attempt to reroute his thoughts.

"The doctor says his cognitive tests are coming back looking very promising," she said. They'd wheeled him out of the room, promising to bring him back soon. Dalton wished the prognosis on their grandmother was better. She'd been having a difficult time. Much more so than Grandpa Lor. At least there was hope now, which was more than they'd had yesterday. "But it's getting late, and we should think about ordering in food."

"I can swing out and pick something up," he said. "No need to eat more hospital food."

"It wasn't too bad the first few days," Jules said. "But I can't stand the smell of it now." His sister stood there for a long moment. "He's awake, Dalton." Her voice held disbelief and shock rolled up into one.

"It's a miracle," he agreed, still trying to process the news. He'd bolted out of the courthouse quickly. Part of him felt guilty for not telling Blakely himself, but there'd been no time, and he'd needed to get on the road as quickly as possible.

"Don't take this the wrong way, but is everything okay?" Jules asked. "You seem distracted."

"I'm good," he said. "*Shock* is probably a better word for what I'm feeling right now." It was mostly true. There were other feelings mingled with regret.

Jules's gaze shifted to a spot behind Dalton's left shoulder. Her forehead wrinkled in confusion. "Someone is headed toward us, and her gaze is fixated on the back of your head. Should we be concerned?"

Dalton turned in time to see Blakely making a beeline straight toward him. Threads of hair had freed themselves from her slicked-back ponytail. Half of her white shirt was untucked from her navy pencil skirt. He blinked a couple of times to make sure he wasn't hallucinating. "What are you doing here?"

Jules cleared her throat and introduced herself to Blakely. "I'm Dalton's sister."

"I've heard about you," Blakely said, offering a handshake.

"Really?" Jules asked, wide-eyed. His sister needed to

get better about hiding her surprise when she was caught off guard by a comment. "Well, it's good to meet you." She turned to Dalton. "I'll run out for burgers. Do you still like the usual?"

"Yes," he said, pulling out a credit card and handing it to his sister. "But only if you let me pay."

"Can I get you anything?" Jules asked Blakely, ignoring him.

"No, thank you," she responded.

"Put that away," Jules said with a wrinkled nose before excusing herself and making an exit. That was Jules. She had a dramatic flair.

"You didn't answer my question," he said to Blakely.

"I heard there was a family emergency, and I was afraid something... How are your grandparents, by the way?" she asked.

"My grandfather woke up," he said. "Apparently, he just sat up and asked for my grandmother's potato soup. Said he was starving."

"And your grandmother?"

He shook his head. "There's been no change." It dawned on him that no one followed Blakely out of the elevator. "Where is your protection?"

"I'm sorry about your grandmother, but that's incredible news about your grandfather." She ignored the question.

"Thank you," he responded, then repeated the question, slower this time.

"Nice guy," she said. "I ditched him." She made a move to enter his grandmother's room. "Are visiting hours over?"

Did she think he was going to gloss over that response? "Not for family. And why the hell did you think taking off without protection was a good idea?"

"I didn't." She lowered her voice, fisted her right hand

and then planted it on her hip. "In fact, I didn't think at all. You were gone, and I didn't know if you were okay. So I slipped out the back, and Ralph drove me to my car. I had to check on you."

She'd been clear where he stood with her. Did she need a reminder?

"My supervisor is probably popping TUMS over this incident," he said through clenched teeth. "Coming here on your own is reckless, Blakely. Or have you forgotten that someone out there is trying to kill you?" He fished his cell out of his pocket.

"I needed to know that you were okay," she said. "Now that I have, I can go."

As she tried to stalk past, Dalton grabbed her wrist to stop her. Skin-to-skin contact wasn't his brightest idea. The sizzle of electricity nearly lit a fire. "Don't. Go."

She lifted her gaze to meet his.

"It's not safe for you to leave by yourself," he clarified. The last thing he wanted to do was give her hope. She'd crushed any fantasy he'd had about the possibility of the two of them being more than professional associates. "You get that, right?"

She compressed her lips and nodded.

"You have to take this threat seriously," he continued, firing off a text to his supervisor to let him know she was safe. The move might get him in more trouble, but it was the right thing to do.

"You don't think I am?"

"Ditching the person sworn to protect you isn't a good move, Blakely."

There was so much hurt and disappointment in her eyes that a knot tightened in his chest. Damn. He needed to get a grip.

"I SHOULDN'T HAVE come here." Blakely had made a huge mistake. It was clear to her now that Dalton had been doing his job and didn't want to see her again. As far as the couple of kisses went—kisses that had more promise than any she'd had before meeting him—he most likely got caught up in the moment. Besides, she'd been the initiator, and he'd been along for the ride.

When she put it like that, it didn't sound a bit like Dalton's personality. But it was easier to stick him in that bucket than face the fact she'd let a good person go because of fears she couldn't seem to conquer.

"You're here," he said, all business now. "You might as well stick around until someone can be sent for you."

His cell buzzed. He checked the screen and then excused himself to take the call.

While he was gone, Blakely sent the message to clear her docket for the rest of the week due to her personal safety being compromised. Johnny Spear, or whoever had been behind the wheel of the SUV that had rammed into her, would be able to set up on a nearby rooftop and make the shot as she walked up the courthouse stairs.

Disappearing for a minute to give authorities time to find him and catch him made the most sense to her now. But where could she go? She should have considered this before hopping into the car on a whim. Blakely didn't do "whim." She'd never done "whim."

What had gotten into her?

The short answer? Dalton Remington. He was a game changer. One she couldn't afford.

Speaking of the devil, he came walking up.

"How is your sister?" he asked after tucking the cell inside his pocket.

"Stable," she said. "Greg and Chase should already be

with her this evening. She's sitting up and able to talk on the phone. We had a good conversation on the drive over." Blakely issued a sharp sigh. "Looks like we're both getting positive news tonight." She wasn't sure how he would react to what she wanted to say next. "Would it be all right if I went inside the room and met your grandmother?"

"There a reason?" he asked.

"I'd like to be your friend," she said. "If that option is ever on the table. And if it isn't, then we both walk away once this is over."

"After you," he said with a small nod and a ghost of a smile on his lips—lips that she didn't need to focus on.

The room was softly lit. The steady beep of machines next to his grandmother's bed that were much like a heartbeat reassured her.

There were flowers and cards on every surface. The room smelled of lilacs and roses. "Wow." There was so much love surrounding this woman.

Who would care if Blakely was gone?

Her sister and Chase. At one time, she would have added Greg's name to the list, but she barely recognized her brother-in-law anymore. At her gravesite, there would be exactly two people.

How sad was that? And why did she suddenly care? She'd gotten by fine until now taking care of her sister and Chase. Wanting more out of life aside from her small family and work came out of the blue.

"I don't think it was the smartest idea to ditch your protection and drive here on your own," Dalton whispered. "But I'm glad you made it safely."

"My car took a hit, but I'm okay." She regretted the words the second they left her mouth. "Before you jump on me again, it happened in my neighborhood before I could get to the highway, and I called it in."

"Johnny Spear?" he asked, the corners of his mouth turning down in a frown.

"I couldn't get a good look at the SUV driver, but I assumed it was him," she said. "Who else would it be?"

Concern lines creased his forehead. "Did Houston PD report back?"

"As far as I know, he's still on the loose," she said.

"Consider me back on your case," he said under his breath.

"Is that a good idea?"

"Do you have a better one?" he quipped, raking fingers through his hair. He paced back and forth in front of the window.

"I haven't really thought about it," she admitted. "Ralph was able to keep me safe out the back of the courthouse, and he was the one who made sure I was behind the wheel with doors locked before he even thought about leaving."

"Johnny Spear could have followed you from the courthouse or been waiting for another opportunity to strike at your house."

"That's the reason I took Ralph with me," she tried to explain.

"Not good enough, Blakely. You could have been killed." The pacing quickened.

"But I wasn't," she said, trying to soothe him. As it was, she could almost see the wheels spinning as he retreated in thought. "I'm here. I'm in one piece. And I can't spend my whole life worrying about 'what if' because that would push me over the edge. A lot can happen. It didn't. I'm safe."

"Promise me that you won't disappear," he stated. "I'll request to be put back on your case, but you have to give me your word that you won't do anything to jeopardize your own safety."

Blakely raised her right hand. "Do you have a stack of Bibles?"

Because she was ready to take an oath that she would stay by Dalton's side and allow him to protect her.

Could she trust him with her heart?

Chapter Eighteen

The text came through approving Dalton's request to be reinstated on Blakely's case in a matter of minutes.

Are you sure this is what you want?

His response was direct: Never been more certain of anything in my life, boss.

Done.

Dalton glanced up at Blakely, who he was surprised to learn had been studying him like notes the night before a final. "I'm back on the case. You're my responsibility now, and I take my job seriously."

"So I've noticed," she shot back as she matched his glare. "You're the best. It's the reason I'm still alive, and I don't take that for granted."

"No more funny business. Period. Understand?"

Blakely looked more than a little put off by the comment.

"I have no intention of getting myself killed," she lobbed back with fire in her eyes. "And I feel a whole lot better with someone who I know is competent having my back than a stranger who is punching a time card." Daggers shot from her eyes now. "And no more funny business on your side either."

It wasn't the words she said so much as the way she'd said them that had him thinking she'd changed topics on him. Did she mean the couple of kisses they'd shared? Because he hadn't been the one to initiate them. Though, he'd been a willing participant. No way in hell could he regret those, or even stick them in the category of *bad ideas*. They were. But they'd also been the best kisses of his life and had held the most heat and promise. He knew exactly what happened next when he let those kisses run wild. Primal instinct took on a life of its own when his hands roamed her smooth, silky skin. She was the closest thing to heaven on earth he'd ever experienced, and he highly doubted he would ever have the pleasure of experiencing anything that came remotely close again.

"We're in agreement then," he said vaguely. Two could play games. Speak in veiled sentences. "No more."

Before Dalton could issue another response, he saw Grandpa Lor being wheeled toward him after the elevator doors closed.

Seeing his grandfather alert and alive filled him with emotion. Dalton's heart was so full it could burst open.

Blakely followed his gaze and turned around, and he could see a warm smile spread across what had been a serious face only a few seconds ago. "The family resemblance is strong."

"That's my grandfather, all right." Dalton had barely finished his sentence when his feet started moving of what felt like their own volition toward his grandfather, not stopping until he was bent over the wheelchair in a warm embrace. This was almost too good to be true after fearing too much time had passed with his grandfather in a coma for him to make a meaningful recovery.

There was something about seeing his grandfather that

seemed to wash away all his anger and frustration from a few moments ago.

Blakely had taken a huge risk in coming to the hospital. The small but annoying voice in the back of his head reminded him that she'd taken that risk *to be with him* and *to make sure he was okay*. There was no way he could stay angry at her for risking her own life to see him.

He wasn't ready to assign a meaning to it either, like she was in love with him and unable to see it or cop to the fact.

"Welcome back, Grandpa Lor. Welcome back." Dalton whispered those words on repeat in his grandfather's ear.

"It's good to be back," Grandpa Lor admitted.

Sizing him up, Dalton could tell he'd lost a few pounds, but it wasn't anything Mama Bea's country-fried steak couldn't fatten up.

"Grandpa, I'd like you to meet my friend Blakely."

Blakely stepped forward and extended a hand. "It's my pleasure to have the honor of meeting you."

Grandpa Lor's gaze shifted from Blakely to Dalton and back. He said, "I'd be proud to shake your hand. However, we're huggers in the Remington family."

That was all he had to say for Blakely to close the distance between them and offer a warm hug.

A dozen campfires lit inside Dalton's chest at seeing two of the most important people in his life hugging.

"I've heard a lot about you," Blakely said.

"Don't believe any of it. I'm not nearly so wild as the rumors would have you believe." Grandpa Lor winked. His usual lightness and sense of humor was intact. His mind was sharp. For the first time since this whole ordeal began, Dalton had real hope life might return to some semblance of normal. Grandma Lacey had to pull through. Life wouldn't be the same without her.

Blakely's wide smile as she practically beamed at his grandfather sent another jolt of electricity straight to Dalton's heart.

The nurse behind the wheelchair, gripping the handles, cleared her throat. "I hate to be the one to break up this family reunion, but we are in the hallway, and I'd like to get Mr. Remington back into his room so I can get him more comfortable in his bed."

Dalton and Blakely stepped aside at the exact same moment, parting like the Red Sea to allow the nurse to wheel Grandpa back inside the room.

As Grandpa passed Dalton, he reached for his hand and asked, "Has there been any change with my girl since I was gone?" If Dalton was ever going to commit his life to anyone, he would want to have the kind of love story his grandparents had. High school sweethearts turned life partners who'd built a small business from the ground up together. Ranching was hard work, and yet he never once heard his grandparents complain. Then again, complaining wasn't in their nature.

"No, sir," Dalton said, the nurse agreeing a moment later.

She added, "But just like you, Mrs. Remington's condition could change at any minute now. You hang on to that. You hear?" Dalton heard the hopefulness in the nurse's voice and wished he felt the same way when it came to his grandmother. Having Grandpa Lor back was nothing short of a miracle. Did he dare hope for a second?

Dalton instinctively reached for Blakely's hand and linked their fingers as they followed the wheelchair inside his grandmother's room. He told himself the physical connection with Blakely made him breathe easier because he didn't want to let her out of his sight and not because her touch comforted him in ways he knew better than to allow.

He wanted to know that she was always near so he could keep an eye on her. She needed to be within arm's reach at all times should anything serious go down.

They'd barely walked into the room when Dalton's cell buzzed. He fished it out of his pocket and checked the screen. "It's from Jules."

"Is everything okay?" Blakely asked.

"Yes, she's fine," he said. "She's asking for help to bring up all the food from the parking lot."

The thought of leaving his grandfather even for a few minutes docked a boulder on the center of his chest. What if he left and his grandpa Lor fell back into a coma? He'd just gotten him back.

Blakely, who was standing right next to him, nudged him with her elbow. Then she whispered, "I'll go down. You stay here with your grandfather."

Dalton bit back the urge to say no. Because this was Jules they were talking about. She was also a highly trained and damn good US marshal. And his sister wouldn't let anything happen to Blakely any more than he would.

"Okay," he agreed. "Thank you."

"I'll be right back," Blakely promised. He let go of her hand before he changed his mind. Besides, he never would have agreed if she hadn't outsmarted Johnny Spear to show up here in the first place. The fact she'd risked her life to come see Dalton wasn't lost on him. But he couldn't afford to let himself get wrapped up in the gesture.

Besides, he needed to help his grandfather out of the wheelchair and into the bed. Dalton moved beside the nurse. "I can lend a hand."

"That would be appreciated," she said.

This close, Dalton could assess just how much weight his grandfather had lost. Hoisting the man up was too easy. He stood on spindly legs, but that wasn't anything good Southern cooking couldn't fix.

"I'll leave you to it," the nurse said after reconnecting Grandpa Lor to the machines next to his bed. She paused at the door. "Lori-Anna has been calling every day to check on you and your wife. Am I allowed to call her back and give her a status update on your condition?"

Dalton hadn't heard his mother's name spoken out loud in longer than he could remember. He had no desire to see or hear from her again after what she'd pulled. Even hearing it now, after all these years, caused his hands to fist at his sides. What could possess a person to walk out on their infant son? Not to mention another son and daughter who were barely old enough to wipe their own backsides? She'd walked out on her husband and her children. Dalton had no use for the woman, despite the tug of curiosity deep in his chest.

"You have my permission to tell Lori-Anna about my status and tell her that I appreciate her calling and checking on me," Grandpa Lorenzo said, much to Dalton's complete shock and horror. Then added, "I'll give her a call as soon as I'm able."

He waited for the nurse to exit before he pulled a seat next to Grandpa Lor's bed and asked, "Do you really want that woman to receive an update, or are you just being kind?"

Grandpa Lor studied Dalton for a long moment. He motioned toward a big white pitcher with a straw poking out of the top next to his bed that was probably filled with ice water.

Dalton handed it over carefully.

After taking a sip, Grandpa Lor cleared his throat and said, "Your mother's situation was complicated. I understand why you wouldn't want to talk about her, so we didn't force the conversation on any of you."

"Does that mean you stayed in touch with her over the years?" Dalton asked, a hornet's nest of emotions buzzing around his heart. As angry as he still was, curiosity was getting the best of him. After almost losing his grandfather and with the possibility still looming that he could lose Grandma Lacey, his heart must have softened when it came to blood ties.

No. The subject was dead, and he should probably leave it alone.

"I won't pretend to condone what Lori-Anna did all those years ago," Grandpa Lor began. Speaking caused him to cough. He paused long enough to take another sip of water before holding the big jug in his once sturdy, now shaky hands. "Life is complicated. Families are complicated. Sometimes, finding a place of understanding is better than holding on to anger."

Dalton couldn't remember a time when either of his grandparents spoke ill about anyone in the family. His no-good uncle had ditched Dalton's cousins after his wife died. The good son, Dalton's father, had been killed in an accident on the ranch. His wife had walked out on their children a couple of years before his death.

So, yeah, he completely understood just how complicated families can be. Relationships fell into the same boat. He'd be a hypocrite if he said otherwise. Especially considering his relationship with Blakely. Or lack of relationship, he should say.

"I know it's probably hard for you to understand," Grandpa Lor continued before another small coughing jag.

"Maybe you should rest," he said, not wanting to wear his grandfather out.

"I'd rather talk, if that's all right with you," Grandpa Lor said. "I've been asleep too long, and it feels good to have company."

"All right then," Dalton said.

"Your mother had a lot of difficulty after you were born," Grandpa Lor said. "No one understood what was happening at the time, including her. Times were different almost thirty years ago. Difficulties were swept under the rug. She went inside herself. Got real quiet. Which wasn't anything like her normal personality."

"Does that excuse what she did in everyone's eyes?" Dalton couldn't help the question.

"I never said it did," Grandpa Lor said wistfully. "I think sometimes it helps to understand, even if it doesn't excuse someone's behavior, if that makes sense."

"It does," Dalton confirmed, not yet ready to let go of his feelings toward the woman who birthed him but couldn't stand to stick around long enough to raise him. She hadn't tried to reach out since then either. Not one birthday card over the years. Not one Christmas present. As a young boy, Dalton couldn't count the number of times he'd fantasized that he would wake up Christmas morning, run downstairs and find her sitting next to the Christmas tree with an armful of presents.

Too many.

Don't get him started on all the birthdays he'd spent waiting by the phone just in case she called. He'd wasted a lot of energy and a lot of time waiting for his mother to make an appearance. He'd cried himself to sleep as a little boy, wishing he had a mother like the other kids on the playground had.

And then one night, he made a promise to himself never to shed another tear.

That was the last time he'd cried.

"Time doesn't heal every wound," Grandpa Lor said.

It occurred to Dalton that he'd been talking to Grandpa for several minutes. Blakely should be back by now. He checked his cell. Nothing.

"Excuse me while I send a message to Jules, Grandpa," Dalton said.

Grandpa Lor gave the okay via a quick nod before he took another sip of water.

Dalton sent the text. Checked the time stamp on the one Jules had sent. It came in twelve minutes ago. *Fourteen minutes.*

The parking lot was a two-minute walk from the ER. There wasn't a lot of activity at the hospital today, so the elevators shouldn't take long. A bad feeling settled in his chest.

Panic slammed into him with the force of a two-by-four. Where were they? Where was Blakely?

Chapter Nineteen

An arm came around Blakely as she approached the second row in the parking lot.

"Got you, bitch." It was the same voice from the other night. She was certain of it. She searched her memory bank for what Johnny Spear's voice had sounded like and came up without a match. Nothing made sense as a band tightened around her body, pinning her arms to her side.

Blakely tried to throw an elbow into her attacker's midsection. The band tightened.

The light closest to her was out. A glow in the distance was far to make anything out by.

She wondered why Jules was still sitting in the driver's seat, facing forward. *Oh no.* Please don't let it be that something bad had happened to Jules. She wasn't moving. It was like a mannequin sat in the driver's seat instead of a real person. This situation was bad.

Blakely would never forgive herself if she got Dalton's sister killed because of her actions. But she couldn't focus on that right now. Not while this man's grip was around her like a vise, making movement impossible.

She *had* to break free. Blakely attempted to jerk her arms free.

No use.

He was strong. Too strong.

She attempted to drop down, forcing her legs to become rubber.

No use.

The trick didn't work. She needed to think. *Think. Think.*

Blakely couldn't get a good look at the attacker since he'd come from behind. She tried to memorize details about him. He had no particular smell that she could identify like a cologne or the stench of cigarettes. There was no alcohol smell either.

What else?

The man was tall. Roughly six feet. That much she could tell. Otherwise, he had on something thick, a hoodie. She could see the thick cotton material on his arm even in the darkness.

Struggling against her arm restraints, she tried to squirm out of the man's grip.

Once again, to no avail.

"Take this," he said in a growl.

The next thing she knew, a hard object slammed into the crown of her head.

The urge to vomit caused bile to rise up the back of her throat. She swallowed and tried to focus blurry eyes as she was being ushered toward Jules's vehicle.

Once again, she tried to fight.

"Hold still," the man growled.

Another blow to the back of her head made her dizzy. It hit with such force that her teeth rattled. A dark cloud was closing in over her brain, but she knew better than to give in to it. She knew 100 percent that she would be dead before she ever opened her eyes again if she allowed the darkness that was threatening to close around her like a heavy cloak.

No way in hell did this sonofabitch get to win. Not as long as she had air in her lungs.

She had to make a move. It was now or never.

Blakely fought like a wild banshee, pushing against the tight grip around her arms.

"I got you," came the voice. "You won't get away this time." There was so much anger and frustration in a voice that was so unfamiliar to her. "You'll pay for scratching me up before, honey."

Her next thought was this bastard had scared her nephew into hiding. Anger fired through her, giving her a boost of adrenaline. With it, she mounted another fight. This man had the strength of an ox. Fighting was no use.

So she screamed at the top of her lungs.

There was no one around in the parking lot, but she expected Jules to turn her head. When she didn't, all hope Dalton's sister might still be alive was dead. This animal had just murdered a US marshal. He would think nothing of doing the same thing to a judge.

Her thoughts immediately turned to Dalton and what losing his sister would do to him. It would destroy him, and she would be responsible for bringing this tragedy to his doorstep. It was her fault.

Blakely screamed again, more out of frustration than anything else.

Because no one came in or out of the doors on this side of the parking lot. It was getting late in a town that rolled up its streets by eight o'clock every night.

"Shut your mouth," Hoodie ordered.

The man was going to kill her.

Her first thought might have been about Dalton, but her second was for Bethany and Chase. How would her sister survive without Blakely's help? What would happen to Chase? His family was already falling apart as it was. She couldn't let him lose his aunt.

Renewed determination to live filled her.

"Who are you? And what do you want from me?"

"Honey, you're my meal ticket. Nothing more," he said in a chilling tone. Those words, spoken with such detachment, sent chills racing up her spine.

Two words stuck out. *Meal. Ticket.* Was it possible someone had hired this man to "handle" her? Could she get this bastard to talk? Maybe trip him up? She had a law degree for heaven's sake. Maybe she could use it to her advantage.

"You want money?" she asked. "How much is my life worth to you?"

"I—uh," the man stuttered. "Just shut your trap, honey."

The word *honey* was the equivalent of fingernails on a chalkboard to her.

"No. It's only fair if you're going to kill me for money to give me a chance to buy my way out of it. I have a lot of money. Are you sure the person who's paying you does?"

"He does just fine."

"How do you know?" If she could just plant a few seeds of doubt in this man's mind, maybe she could talk her way out of this.

"Shut up!" His tone was final. She didn't like the panic in his voice or the anger. Her tactic could backfire on her and cause him to put a knife in her back right now, leaving her for dead like Dalton's sister.

Speaking of murder, why didn't this bastard just shoot her from a distance and leave her for dead?

Did he want to take her to a different location so he could dump her body or scrub it?

Had Jules gotten in the way?

None of this was encouraging, but she needed to dissect the situation and search for an out. One thing was certain, this man meant business. He was very clear about that.

"You need to go to sleep," he whispered before another blow practically knocked her teeth loose. The next strike was harder than the first and hit the same spot at the crown of her head. What had he used?

The butt of a gun or possibly a knife handle?

His one arm, wrapped around her like a band, was stronger than both of hers put together. Now that he'd picked her up and was holding her to one side, could she throw her head back and cause the man some pain at the very least?

Get some of her DNA on him? Or his underneath her nails?

Screaming in the isolated parking lot wasn't doing any good. She had to try something.

DALTON KNEW SOMETHING was wrong. He fired off a text to his sister, asking what was going on and what was taking them so long. Then he waited. A minute passed with no response.

"What is it?" Grandpa Lor asked. "What's wrong?"

Dalton shook his head. "She should have been back by now. And Jules isn't returning my text. Something's off."

Dalton looked up and caught Grandpa Lor's stare. The second their eyes connected, Grandpa Lor's expression said he knew exactly what Dalton was talking about. Once a marshal, always a marshal. Those instincts never went away.

"Go get your girls."

Dalton nodded before standing up and rushing toward the hallway. He stopped at the door and looked back. It did the soul good to see his grandfather awake and alert.

He tapped the doorjamb a couple of times. "Watch out for anything suspicious while I'm gone, okay?"

Grandpa Lor reached toward the call button. "It isn't much, but it should stir up a bee's nest of attention should the need arise." His mischievous smile was back, and it warmed Dalton's heart to see its return.

Dalton offered a small smile before making a beeline toward the elevator bank.

Blakely could be anywhere, but his money was on the parking lot since Jules hadn't returned his texts. The thought of anything happening to his sister was enough to cause his hands to fist. Add Blakely to the mix, and he was downright boiling over.

You should have gone down instead. The voice of shame shot daggers straight through his heart. Guilt consumed him. He should have been the one to run down to pick up the food. Now, he'd not only put Blakely in danger but his sister too.

If anything had happened to Jules...

Nope. He couldn't go there. Not until he assessed the situation.

But he had no time to deflect the shame as he tapped the elevator button for a third time in a row. Would constantly hitting the button make the metal machine move toward him faster? He didn't know and didn't care. It gave him something to do with his hands while he waited. Besides, his tombstone would never read: *Here lies a patient man.*

The elevator dinged and then the doors opened. His chest squeezed when it came up empty. He wanted Blakely and Jules to step out of that elevator and tell him what a worrier he was. He wanted to be wrong about the pair of them being in trouble. He wanted, no, *needed*, both of them to be safe.

Instincts honed by years of experience said he was about to find out just how badly he'd misjudged the situation. And he would never forgive himself for the mistake.

Chapter Twenty

Blakely brought her hands up to dig through the layer of thick cotton and find her attacker's skin. She managed to maneuver enough to slip a hand underneath the material of his hoodie, up the sleeve. It was then she realized he was wearing some type of rubber glove just like the other night. So he was still concerned about leaving any DNA traces behind.

This was no doubt the same person who'd attacked her before. He must have been following her up to now, biding his time. Was he the same person who'd driven the SUV?

The short answer was most likely *yes*.

If this man was going to kill her in this parking lot, she fully intended to have some of his DNA under her fingernails.

Blakely made a claw shape with her hand before digging her nails deep into the flesh of his wrist and then scraping as far as she could go.

Hoodie bit out a few choice words but didn't loosen his grip.

She needed to break free. She needed to get loose. What could she do to stop this bastard from killing her?

Now that she was approaching the vehicle, she saw Jules's face muscle twitch. She was alive?

A burst of hope filled Blakely's chest. Dalton's sister was alive!

The realization gave her a boost. After bringing her chin to her chest, she threw her head back in one quick motion, connecting the back of her skull with his left jaw. A crack sounded as pain shot through her and a trickle ran down the back of her neck. Blood?

Better his than hers. However, she didn't connect with his nose. His jaw wouldn't bleed.

The blood had to belong to her.

Closing in on Jules's vehicle, Blakely wondered what this man had done to the marshal to make her sit so still. Until she got close enough to see the look of panic in Jules's eyes and the beads of sweat trickling down the side of her face.

"What the hell have you done to her?" she demanded.

Hoodie chuckled. The evil sound vibrated through her.

"You will behave from here on out, or she'll go *boom*." Those words cut through Blakely with the precision of a knife.

A bomb.

Jules was strapped to a bomb. It made sense now why she wasn't so much as turning her head despite the fact she had to know they were coming at her from the driver's side, and they were only a foot or two from the door. Jules's gaze was focused forward. Tension tightened the muscles of her neck and shoulders like an overstrung cello.

Now it made sense.

Icy fingers of panic gripped Blakely's chest.

"I'm the one you want. Let her go," she reasoned.

"Not a chance," he said with amusement. This was funny to him? The man was comfortable killing others, so he was most likely a lifetime criminal.

"How much are you being paid?" she asked for the second time.

"More than you can afford." His voice raked through her. "This is your own fault. You had to fight back, didn't you? Now you're a liability."

What the hell did that mean?

A liability?

Wasn't she the intended target?

"You have no idea how much money I have or what I'm capable of," she shot back. Keeping him talking was a stall tactic. He didn't seem to realize she was giving Dalton time to miss them and wonder what had happened.

Would he figure it out too late?

"You messed everything up, and now you have to pay," Hoodie said through clenched teeth. She'd hoped to crack a molar with the backward headbutt. Give him a fraction of the pain he was causing. "And you need to go to sleep so you can't cause any more trouble."

"The woman sitting in the car is a US marshal," she said out of desperation..

"And you're a judge," he snapped. "So what? Neither one of you are in control now, are you?"

Blakely made mental notes just in case by some miracle she survived. He was someone who resented the legal system. Someone who'd done time? Possibly with Johnny Spear?

She didn't recognize him as someone she'd sentenced, but that didn't mean much considering her caseload.

"Johnny's broke," she said in the equivalent of throwing spaghetti against the wall to see if it stuck. "I don't care what he promised you. He won't be able to deliver. I'm worth nothing, and you'll go to jail for him."

"You're right about one thing," he said before adding, "You're worthless. In the way."

In the way.

Of what? A payoff?

"And I don't know who this Johnny person is, but if he hates you, he's doing just fine in my book."

Now Blakely really was confused.

Why attack her if she wasn't the real intended target? Had someone made a mistake? Ended up in her driveway when they were meant to be somewhere else? And now what? She could identify someone in a lineup, so she couldn't be allowed to live?

No. That didn't make any sense either.

"Look, you're about to kill me anyway," she started, wondering how much information she could get from Hoodie. "Why don't you just tell me who is behind this? Why not let me know the name of the person who is having me killed? Don't I deserve to know that much before I die?"

Hoodie issued a disgusted grunt.

Wrong tactic.

"Or don't you believe you can get the job done, so you have to protect yourself?" Based on the fact he got really quiet, she realized she'd struck a nerve. Taunting him was risky, but the bigger risk was doing nothing and letting him carry out her murder. "Oh, you're not authorized to say, are you? You're just a pawn. The sacrifice should this whole thing go south. You're the one who goes to jail when the law comes after you for my murder, and believe me, they will. I already have plenty of your DNA underneath my fingernails. My murder will be connected to you. Law enforcement will hunt you down like a hunter stalks a feral hog. You're already in the database anyway. Your biometrics have been taken because you've already served time."

His grip tightened around her. She was scoring direct hits. Now to keep it going but not push so far that she shoved him over the edge, and he snapped her neck in half. She had no doubt he was strong enough to do exactly that with his bare hands.

He was angry enough to crack.

Blakely took in a slow, deep breath. If she couldn't overpower Hoodie physically, she had to win on a different level…the mental game.

"How do you plan to kill me anyway?" she continued.

"Boom!" he whispered as he walked her to the passenger door. "Get in."

This was so not good.

Blakely did as instructed, as Hoodie pulled a cell phone out of his pocket and smiled. His hood was on and cinched around his face, revealing precious little of the details of his features.

He held up the cell as he backed away into the darkness.

Blakely glanced over at Jules. "I'm so sorry."

CROUCHED LOW, LIKE A tiger about to strike, Dalton moved through the vehicles without making a sound. He overshot the bastard in the Hoodie who'd been carrying Blakely with one arm so he could come up from behind.

He also assessed the situation and determined there was a bomb either strapped to his sister or in her vehicle. Probably on Jules, if he had to guess.

One wrong move and two of the people he loved would go *boom!*

Dalton couldn't lose anyone else.

So he bided his time as Hoodie backed away. The phone must be linked to the detonator. Again, he was guessing, but it appeared that Hoodie had to tap the screen. He wouldn't do that until he was in the clear.

So Dalton waited.

A little closer.

Like a lion leaping toward a gazelle, Dalton dove at Hoodie, striking him from the side at the knees.

A crack sounded as the big man was knocked off-balance, and his cell flew out of his hand. Dalton flinched, half expecting the bomb to detonate. His moment of relief when it didn't was short-lived as Hoodie landed hard on the pavement and immediately threw a punch. His fist connected with Dalton's chin, causing his head to snap to the left.

The sound of car doors opening and closing broke through the ringing noise in his ears. Before Jules and Blakely could get to him, Hoodie pulled a gun and shoved the barrel on Dalton's right temple.

Dalton muttered a string of curses.

The man was fast.

"Back away or I'll shoot," Hoodie demanded as his gaze searched for his cell.

Hands up, both Jules and Blakely took a couple of steps back.

"Find my cell and give it back to me," he ordered. "Or I'll blow his head off."

"Are you sure you want to do that?" Jules asked, calm as anyone pleased. "Because that man is a US marshal. You'll do hard time."

"They won't catch me again," the man quipped. Had he altered his appearance with surgery? Removed his fingerprints?

There were ways for career criminals to erase the ability to match them in a database using biometrics.

"Stand up," Hoodie said to Dalton. "Now."

Dalton did as ordered, once again waiting for the right moment to strike. He'd taken a calculated risk by attacking Hoodie. Dalton had needed the element of surprise in order to stop him from tapping the screen and blowing up Jules and Blakely.

He hadn't anticipated the man recovering so quickly. Or being able to access his gun so quickly. But the risk had paid off. Jules and Blakely were safely out of the vehicle, and nothing had blown up.

"I think I see your phone," Jules said. "I'm going to walk over and pick it up."

"Walk slow," Hoodie demanded.

"Okay," she said. "You can watch me as I go." She took a few steps away from them then bent down. "It's underneath this vehicle. Okay? I'm going to crawl on all fours so I can retrieve it. Are we still good?"

"Yes," he said. "But do anything that makes me nervous, and I'll blow his head off."

"I got it," Jules said calmly before doing exactly what she'd said. "Bad news." She backed up and then sat on her heels. "Phone's shattered."

Hoodie cursed as she held up the screen so he could verify what she said was fact.

"Put your hands on the vehicle where I can see 'em," he demanded.

Jules stood up and did as he said.

Hoodie looked at Blakely next. "You do the same thing on the car next to her."

Blakely held her hands high in the air where he could see them.

The sound of sirens wailed in the distance.

The next thing Dalton knew, he felt a blow and then nothing.

By the time he came to again, he was in a hospital room, and his head felt like it had been split in two with an axe.

"He didn't act alone," Jules said as Blakely squeezed his hand. The women stood on opposite sides of the bed. Blakely pulled up a chair while Jules paced in front of the window.

"Do you mind doing that over there?" He pointed to the back wall.

"Oh," Jules said, realizing she was making herself an easy target. "Yes. Good point."

"What happened to him?" he asked Blakely.

She shook her head. "He's gone."

"How did it happen?" he continued, realizing he probably didn't want to know but couldn't help himself.

"The gun he pointed at you convinced us to stay put and count to ten slowly," she explained. "It gave him the head start he needed to disappear."

The gunman had used Blakely and Jules to disarm Dalton.

"What about the bomb?" he asked.

"There's a bomb squad outside right now," Blakely said. "We should be getting word at any moment that it has been defused. At least, that's the hope."

"How long have I been out?"

"Half hour tops," she answered.

Dammit. Dammit. Dammit.

The bastard slipped out of their grasp. At least they were all three alive and well. That counted for something. It was the most important thing. "He didn't kills us when he could have."

"I'm hoping some of what I said got through to him," Blakely said.

"Which is?"

She leaned forward and kissed the back of his hand. "He

was being paid to kill me. I offered more money. When he didn't take the bait, I sowed seeds of doubt as to whether or not the person he's working for could pay up."

"Who would hire someone to kill you?" Dalton asked. "Johnny Spear?"

"I checked into his background and have no idea where he would come up with the money to hire someone to kill a judge," she said.

The price would go up based on the amount of time someone would serve. "Then, who?"

"That's the sixty-four-thousand-dollar question," Blakely said on a sharp sigh.

Chapter Twenty-One

For a few miserable moments down in the parking lot, Blakely feared Hoodie was going to shoot Dalton. A panic attack took hold. It was as though the air had been sucked out of the universe, and she couldn't breathe.

"We chased him, but he was prepared," she explained.

Jules piped in, "The jerk had a motorcycle stashed in between two cars. One of those crotch rockets." She shook her head. "We didn't stand a chance because there was no way I was getting back inside my vehicle." Jules smacked the flat of her hand against the wall. "We could have lost you, Dalton."

"I'm here," he reassured her, plucking at the cotton gown. "I'm good." He assessed his injuries. "Can't say my fashion sense is all that stellar." He cracked a smile, and it broke the thick tension in the room. "Who dressed me in this?"

Blakely raised her hand, feeling the red blush heating her cheeks. "That would be me."

"I helped," Jules broke in.

"Great." Dalton compressed his lips, looking like he had to bite back a snappy comment. "Then, you both must know where my pants are."

Jules looked to Blakely and shrugged her shoulders in dramatic fashion. "Beats me."

Blakely laughed. She couldn't help herself. Her relationship with Bethany had never been this light, this playful. This fun?

"Maybe you should hit that call button," Blakely said. "Ask one of the nurses."

"Okay, funny guys," Dalton said, putting his hands in the surrender position. "For the record, I've never felt better."

Jules nodded. "Sure. Is that why you squint when you look at me?"

"So I need glasses," he quipped. "Doesn't everyone at some point?"

"It's late, Dalton." His sister walked over to his bedside. "What do you think about staying put for the night and regrouping in the morning? This day feels like it will never end, and you know how I get when I'm running on E."

"Since I'd planned on spending the night at the hospital anyway, that's not such a bad idea," he conceded, much to Blakely's surprise. He shifted his gaze to her. "Will you stay here too?"

"I don't have anything with me," she said, unable to think up a better argument against the idea. "Not even a toothbrush."

Jules sized her up. "You look to be about my size. If you don't mind sharing my clothes, I always have an emergency overnight bag with me. I left one in Grandpa Lor and Grandma Lacey's room just in case I got permission to stay the night."

"Sounds good," Blakely said. "Besides, my adrenaline rush dissipated a while ago, and crawling into bed sounds amazing right now."

"Great. I'll be right back." Jules gave a little wave before disappearing into the hallway. The woman had a remarkable resemblance to the actress Blake Lively when she was in her early twenties, great hair included.

Must be nice.

"Do you think the nurses would kick me out of the hospital if I took the bed over there?" She motioned toward the twin on the other side of the curtain that had been drawn back halfway.

"We can probably make some kind of arrangement," he said. "Or you could just crawl into my bed."

"We both know where that would end up." She couldn't deny the pull toward Dalton or the fact even thinking of being that close to him lit all kinds of wildfires inside her. But it would be a mistake.

"I'm not complaining," he said before shaking his head. "No. Never mind. We've done that dance. Haven't we?"

"We have," she said, not mentioning the part about it being the best dance of her life. Or that she wished more than anything she could figure out a way to trust men. Trust him.

"No use beating a dead horse, in a manner of speaking," he clarified.

"Nope." Even though her lips still burned with the imprint of his from the kisses they'd shared. She needed to change the subject before heat consumed her. "He won't come back tonight. Will he?"

"This guy is unpredictable," he said after a thoughtful pause. "I have no idea what the man is capable of." He paused another beat. "I would never believe someone would go after two marshals and a judge. You, of all people, know the kind of time he would do for that."

"The promised paycheck must be big," she reasoned. "For him to take that kind of risk."

"Who would have that kind of money?" he asked.

"That's a good question." Before Blakely could think too much about it, Jules came bounding into the room again.

"Everything you need should be in this bag." Jules held out the black gym bag.

Blakely took the offering and thanked her.

"I'm going home to grab a couple hours of shut-eye, but should be back at sunrise," Jules said before exchanging goodbyes and then leaving once again.

True to Jules's word, the bag had everything she might need for the evening. "Do you think we should ask permission for me to stay overnight?"

"Nah," Dalton said. "We should be fine."

"Do you need to shower?" she asked.

"Are you offering?"

Blakely's cheeks heated once again. It wasn't a terrible idea. But sex with Dalton would only leave her wanting more. And then what? The whole question of a relationship would enter her mind, causing even more confusion. She couldn't risk it. "I can hit the 'call' button for you if you'd like." She smirked. "Maybe one of the nurses with big, calloused hands will be on duty."

His laugh was a low rumble in his chest, and it was one of the sexiest sounds she'd ever heard. "One can only hope."

Blakely tightened her grip on the handle of the bag and then disappeared into the bathroom. A quick shower did the trick. Brushing her teeth with a clean, fresh toothbrush was beyond amazing.

She'd run out so fast from Houston that she hadn't thought of necessities like clean underwear or toiletries. After getting ready for bed, she brought the bag with her into Dalton's room. He was already asleep, softly snoring.

After climbing into bed, she did her best to shut down her thoughts as they spiraled. Who could hate her so much they wanted her dead? Who would be willing or able to pay someone to erase her?

The same hamster wheel of questions spun through her mind. She turned on her side and then punched the pillow in an attempt to get comfortable.

Closing her eyes only served to bring up images of Hoodie. She'd seen his mouth, his thin-lipped sneer. The fact he had day-old stubble on his chin. She concluded he had dark hair based on his facial hair.

A determined killer stalked her. And she had no idea who or why.

At least she knew the man was someone's puppet.

But who?

THE SECOND DALTON opened his eyes, he checked to see if Blakely was still in the bed next to his. His heart raced until he received visual confirmation that she hadn't taken off while he was out. Then, he could exhale the breath he'd been holding. Still asleep.

As much as he'd wanted to have a relationship with the stunningly beautiful judge, could he ever be certain she wouldn't flip out and take off? Where would that leave him if he was always watching the door to see if she would bolt through it?

A soft knock at the door was followed by Jules entering.

"Good morning," she practically chirped. There'd been a lot of changes in her since Toby. The two had found love and each other while transporting a prisoner. Their chopper went down, and they'd had only each other to rely on. Toby had taken more of the brunt of the injuries and was healing nicely with Jules by his side.

"You've had your fair share of hospital stays of late, haven't you?" he asked as she set down the bag of bagels from his favorite place along with one of those carrying trays that held multiple drinks. This time, there were three cups of coffee.

"Yes," she said on a sigh, taking the seat that had been pulled up next to his bed. "I have. I've been bouncing between floors, but Toby is home now, and Grandpa Lor is awake. It's a miracle. And I never believed in miracles."

"Good to hear Toby is recovering," Dalton said. He should really stop by more often to check on his family members. "When you say *home*. What do you mean?"

"The family ranch," she supplied, taking one of the coffees and handing it to him.

"You're an angel," he said, taking the offering. "I could stand to brush my teeth first."

"Do you need help going to the bathroom?" Jules asked.

"I got it," he said, grasping at the opening in back of his gown before a quick trip to the bathroom. Standing up made him woozy. He needed food in his stomach and caffeine.

"Thanks for the grub," he said as he climbed back under the blanket, tucking in the sides so he didn't accidentally give anyone a peep show.

"You're welcome," she said, taking out a bagel before slathering cream cheese on it.

"I've been thinking a lot lately," he started after she handed it over and he thanked her once again.

"About?"

"Coming back to the ranch," he said.

"I thought you loved your job," Jules said, surprised. She grabbed another bagel and opened it. Everything bagels were manna from heaven.

He acknowledged that he did. "I used to, but things have been changing for me lately. I think I'd like to put in notice and move back to the ranch full-time once this case is over."

"Seriously?" Jules stopped mid-slather.

"I'm dead serious." He regretted his word choice, but the sentiment remained the same. "I've been doing a lot of soul-searching since our grandparents' accident."

"And?"

"Don't you miss the ranch?" he asked.

"Yes, of course," she said. "But that doesn't mean I want to come back and work it full-time." She set down her bagel. "I have been thinking about becoming more involved again though. If I didn't have to give up my job."

"I wonder if everyone else is thinking along the same lines," he said. "Seems like we're usually in sync."

"Crystal would definitely do more," Jules said. "I've been talking to her about it. So would Abilene."

"Have you talked to Camden?"

"Not yet," she said. "He's been unreachable lately. I see that he's been reading the updates. But he doesn't comment."

"I can reach out to him," Dalton said. "Just to get a baseline of what everyone is thinking." He took a bite of bagel, chewed and then followed it with a swig of black coffee. "Grandpa Lor is feisty as usual, but I think he'd be thrilled with the help."

"Did you get a good look at him?" she asked.

Dalton nodded. "He definitely needs some home cooking to put some meat on those bones."

She smiled. "The bagels should help." Then, she added, "I'm proud of you, Dalton. I hope that doesn't sound too mushy or cliché."

He cracked a smile.

"The ranch will be lucky to have you back full-time," she said.

He nodded. "It just feels right. You know?"

"Then you have to do it."

"Any idea how long it'll take Grandpa Lor to be released from the hospital?" he asked.

"Do you seriously think he'll leave Grandma's side?"

"I guess not," he agreed.

"Can you imagine the two of them being separated from each other?"

"No," he admitted. He couldn't. He'd always believed the two of them would ride off into the sunset together. "I doubt death will part them no matter what vows they took on their wedding day."

Jules laughed.

"Agreed," she said before urging him to eat.

Dalton polished off a bagel and then his coffee. "You still haven't told me where they hid my clothes."

"Right. That."

"Do you intend to?" he asked.

"Have you spoken to the doctor about being released?" she asked.

"He stopped by last night after Blakely fell asleep," he said. "Turns out, I have a mild concussion, but I could have told him that."

"You and Camden should know what that feels like after our childhoods," she teased.

"Truer words have never been spoken," he said. "All of us played sports."

"And ran around the ranch like wild animals if memory serves," she added.

He couldn't help but laugh as memories filtered through of him falling out of a tree, Camden falling out of a tree, Duke falling out of a tree. "Our grandparents are saints for putting up with us."

"Yes, they were," she said with a spark in her eyes that he'd seen many times before.

"We had an amazing childhood that I completely took for granted," he said as shame filled him. "I should have been here for them."

"Don't blame yourself, Dalton. Any one of us could say the same thing, and you would be the first to tell us not to think along those lines."

She had a point there. One he couldn't argue.

And then she caught him off guard when she asked, "What about her?" Jules hooked her head in Blakely's direction. "What will happen with your relationship if you move back to Mesa Point?"

"Simple. We don't have a relationship to discuss."

"Really?" Jules asked. "Is that what you think? Because I had no idea my little brother was so oblivious."

Attraction didn't make a relationship, he wanted to point out. And Blakely had been clear about not seeing herself trust another person.

"It takes two to tango, Jules." And he was a one-man show.

Chapter Twenty-Two

"Are those bagels I smell?" Blakely stretched her arms and made a show of waking up. Was she being too obvious? She hadn't intended to eavesdrop on their conversation, but she woke up at "We don't have a relationship to discuss," and it had felt like the wrong time to make it known she could hear.

If not for her bladder forcing her to get out of bed, she would have pretended to be asleep for the rest of their conversation. However, she had to go.

Throwing off the covers, she stepped lightly on the tile flooring.

"Yes," Jules said with a look toward Dalton. "Help yourself."

"Bathroom first," Blakely said before disappearing into the adjacent room. She wished she could crawl through a crack in the wall and disappear after hearing Dalton tell his sister about their non-relationship. Clearly, the woman had picked up on a vibe between Blakely and Dalton.

Were they that obvious?

So much for playing it cool around other people. Blakely couldn't contain her attraction when she was one-on-one with Dalton, but she thought she was doing a decent job of covering in front of others.

Maybe not.

Their chemistry was undeniable. So much for being stealth

about their past. Now, there were questions—questions she couldn't answer. Trying to be with Dalton didn't work. Trying to stay away from Dalton didn't work.

Right now, she was a big ball of contradiction. He must be confused as hell.

Blakely made a quick call to check on her sister before freshening up. Then, she joined the siblings in the next room.

"How'd you sleep?" Jules asked, and Blakely was grateful for the general question. She couldn't answer personal ones right now. Not when she was just as confused as everyone else about the nature of her and Dalton's relationship.

Blakely was handed a bagel and a cup of coffee almost the second she sat down. "Better than anyone should in a hospital."

The comment elicited a couple of laughs and a nod from Dalton, who probably didn't sleep much more than a few minutes here and there.

And then he turned his attention toward his sister.

"Jules, can I ask you a question?" Dalton started before adding, "It's off topic but important."

"Go ahead," she urged. "You know you can ask me anything."

"Did you know about our mother being in contact with our grandparents all these years?" he asked in a direct question.

Jules sat there for a long moment, quiet. She stared out the window and shifted in her seat.

"I did," Jules admitted. She shot a look of apology toward Dalton, who looked like he'd just been betrayed by his best friend.

"Am I the only one who didn't know?" he asked.

"I've never discussed it with Camden," Jules said. "So I can't speak for him."

Based on the look on Dalton's face, the response didn't exactly offer much in the way of reassurance.

"What about her?" he asked. "Are you in touch with her? Do you guys...what?...talk on a regular basis or something?" The rim of his cup suddenly became real interesting to him.

"Not really," Jules admitted.

"What does that mean exactly?" Dalton pressed. "You don't talk at all or don't talk on a regular basis?"

Beep. Beep. Beep. The heart monitor picked up.

Blakely glanced at the machine and then tried to catch Dalton's gaze. No use. His was fixated on his sister.

"Just that," Jules said on a shrug. "I asked our grandparents if they knew anything about our mother for medical history purposes a couple years back." Jules kept her gaze fixed on the window. "Once I opened the door, Grandma Lacey came to me and asked if I had any questions."

"You mean Pandora's box," he quipped. *Beep. Beep. Beep. Beep.*

Jules shot a warning look.

"I'm guessing you did have questions," he continued. *Beep. Beep. Beep.*

"That's right." Jules turned her attention to the sliver of bagel in her hand. She started to take a bite before thinking better of it and setting it down. "My curiosity started with medical questions, and then things spiraled from there. I wanted to know what she was like and if I got any of my traits from her. I look in the mirror, and I don't see a resemblance to Dad. I'm not like you and Cam. I've always felt like I looked like the black sheep of the family and—"

"No way," he countered. "You're *you*. You look like *you*."

Jules pinned him with her gaze. Blakely wouldn't want to go up against Dalton's sister in a bar fight, that was for sure.

"Haven't you ever looked at me and wondered where I got this hair color from?" Jules asked.

"No," he said, shaking his head. "I had no idea you felt that way, or I would have—"

"What? Reassured me?" She blew out a frustrated breath. "And force a discussion about our mother on you and Cam when you both seemed capable of letting a sleeping dog lie?"

"You could have given us the benefit of the doubt that we would have been able to handle talking about her," he pointed out. *Beep. Beep.*

"The subject never came up," Jules admitted. "It's not exactly something we ever discussed. I mean, you and Camden never mentioned anything about our mother, so I guess I figured that you just didn't want to know, and I should leave it alone."

"I'm sorry you didn't feel like you could come to me to talk about it," Dalton said. "I guess I haven't been the easiest person to discuss our parents with."

"Through no fault of your own," she said. "I just figured there would come a day when you would be ready to talk about her or ask questions, and part of me wanted to have the information and be ready should that day ever come. At least, that's another excuse I told myself before I was able to admit that I was just curious where I came from."

"Growing up, you always did put it on yourself to be the one to take care of Cam and I, even though Cam is the oldest," Dalton said.

"He has the most memories of our parents," she said. Blakely wondered if their older brother held on to the most pain too.

"Grandma Lacey did a really great job with all of us," Jules said, twisting her fingers together. This subject obviously made her uncomfortable. "Learning about our mother had nothing to do with the upbringing we had, which was the best."

"Our grandparents did the best they could with the hand they were dealt," Dalton said. "Can you even imagine being at that point in your life and taking on six children?"

Jules shook her head. "I guess I've been thinking about that a lot more lately now that Toby and I..."

Dalton's eyes widened to saucers. "What? Are you telling me that you're—"

"No," Jules said with an expression that made it look like she'd just bitten into a sour grape. The look on her face immediately shut down any notion that she might be pregnant. "We're engaged, not yet married." She paused for a few beats. "I know babies don't necessarily wait, but I've always been on the fence about having children because of our situation."

"I'm not on the fence at all," Dalton stated with finality. "I never intend to have a family."

What was it about that statement—a statement Blakely would have wholeheartedly agreed with a week ago—that caused her stomach to sink and a sense of hopelessness to settle in her chest?

She didn't want a family. Did she?

"Have you met her?" Dalton asked his sister.

"Haven't decided if I want to or can handle it," Jules admitted.

"Grandpa Lor said there's a lot we don't know about our mother's 'situation,' as he called it," Dalton said. "Do you know what he's talking about?"

"I haven't heard anything from her perspective," Jules said. "But I know she was suffering when she left."

"What do you think about setting up a meeting with her to ask questions?" he asked.

"It's crossed my mind," she said. "If only to hear her side of the story. And, I don't know, get closure."

DALTON NOTICED BLAKELY hadn't said a word in several minutes. Then again, he and Jules had been discussing family. He needed to shift gears because he still wasn't sure what to think about his mother being in contact with his grandparents or any member of his family after the stunt she'd pulled. *Anger.* Now, there was a word. *Confused.* It fit.

Was closure possible or a pipe dream?

Either way, Dalton set his empty coffee cup down and turned his attention toward Blakely. "You probably don't want to hear all this about our family."

"I don't mind," she said. He realized she'd lost her parents too. "Families are complicated. I get it. Mine is beyond messy right now."

"Speaking of your family, is there any word on Bethany?"

"My sister lost a lot of blood, so they're keeping her at the hospital after the surgery to remove a bullet fragment from her neck," she explained. "If the bullet hit a few centimeters to the left, there would have been no surviving it."

"It's strange to think of being lucky when you're talking about taking a bullet," Jules conceded. "However, in this case, it sounds like your sister was very lucky."

"She has a lot of thinking to do about her marriage, so being away from home probably isn't the worst thing right now," Blakely continued.

Dalton nodded. "The hospital is secure, and the nurses are watching her room like a hawk."

"There's some peace of mind in that knowledge," Blakely said. Based on the tension lines scoring her forehead, there wasn't much. He understood. If Jules were in a hospital and he couldn't be near... Dalton couldn't even think about it.

Everyone in his family had a dangerous job. Everyone was good at what they did, which didn't rule out the possibility something catastrophic would happen. In order to work the job and sleep at night, he couldn't let himself go there mentally about everything that could go wrong.

"It's not much," he conceded. "Which is why we need to figure out who is behind these attacks so we can put an end to this once and for all."

"As long as Bethany is in the hospital, she's safe," Blakely stated. "Which also buys us some time to figure all this out."

"Speaking of which, I can get a whole lot more done out there than trying to stay in here," he pointed out.

"Hold on there," Jules said. "Where do you think you're going?"

"Out of here," Dalton said firmly.

"What do you think the doctor will say?" Jules asked.

"I think he'll tell me to stop taking up bed space when I'm fine and don't need to be here," Dalton said, a little heated.

"Whoa!" Jules teased. "I'm just trying to be the voice of reason."

"Didn't mean to get riled up," Dalton said.

"Where will we go?" Blakely asked. He liked the fact she wasn't trying to bolt. He'd promised to protect her, and that was exactly what he intended to do.

"My place should be safe," he said.

"That means you have to leave the hospital," Blakely said. He could tell she felt guilty by her expression.

"My grandfather is awake, and we have every reason to believe he'll stay that way," Dalton said.

"You could take Blakely back to the ranch," Jules offered, but both Dalton and Blakely were already shaking their heads before his sister could finish her sentence.

"Too dangerous for everyone else," Blakely said before he could.

"Toby's there, recovering," Jules said. "I'm staying there when I'm not here at the hospital. We'd be ready."

"Someone could light the barn on fire, damage the property or set a blaze just to flush me out of the house," Blakely said. "You already experienced a bomb last night."

"I wasn't ready for it," Jules said a little defensively. Dalton understood how frustrating and embarrassing it was for someone in law enforcement to be tricked. She had nothing to be embarrassed about, but Jules wouldn't see it that way and neither would he if the situation was reversed. Hell, he couldn't forgive himself for letting Blakely go downstairs or not warning Jules of the possibility in the first place.

"It's my fault, not yours," he said to his sister.

"Agree to disagree," Jules said. "But arguing or assigning blame doesn't fix anything."

"Now we agree on something," he said.

"I really hate getting your family involved in any of this mess," Blakely stated.

"We don't," Dalton and Jules said simultaneously.

Dalton added, "It's what we've chosen to do for a living. You're not putting us in any danger that we didn't already sign up for."

Blakely conceded with a slight nod. "This feels more personal."

He knew exactly what she was talking about. Their fling. It made this situation more personal for him too.

There wasn't anything they could do about it now.

"Suffice it to say, I'm not going anywhere until this is resolved," he said, wishing for more but knowing Blakely couldn't give it.

Chapter Twenty-Three

Blakely needed to have a serious conversation with Dalton once this ordeal was over. Right now, all she could think about was keeping everyone safe until law enforcement caught up with the bastard who was determined to kill her.

Her cell buzzed. She checked the screen, and her stomach fell. "It's my brother-in-law."

Locking gazes with Dalton, even for a few seconds, gave her a boost of confidence before she answered the call.

"Hey, Greg. Everything okay?" she asked.

"Aunt Blakely," came Chase's small voice. She listened for any signs of sadness or panic, decided she was searching for something that wasn't there. "Can you come pick me up?"

"Where are you?" she asked.

"Home," Chase said. "I don't like it here without Mommy."

"Are you alone?" she asked.

"Gotta go," Chase whispered. "Daddy's coming."

"Chase?" she asked, but he was already gone. She locked gazes with Dalton. "I need to get back to Houston."

"Is that a good idea?" Dalton asked.

"What choice do I have?"

Dalton seemed at a loss for words.

"Someone bring me up-to-date on what's going on, please," Jules said.

"Blakely just got a call from her nephew," Dalton started.

"Asking me to pick him up," Blakely finished.

"Where?" Jules asked.

"In Houston," Blakely responded.

Jules pushed to standing and started pacing again. "We can get there with some planning."

"I'm sorry to be the one to say this considering I know how much you love your nephew, but you have to consider the possibility you'd be placing him in harm's way," said Dalton.

Right. Like Bethany.

Blakely bit out a curse. "What else am I supposed to do?"

"Catch this bastard so you can get your life back," Dalton said. If only it was that easy.

What if this guy escalated? Then again, he'd tried to blow up her and a US marshal. How much further would this go?

"Chase is safe with his father," Dalton said.

As much as she didn't want to admit it, Dalton was making sense, whereas she was being irrational. Her emotions were at the wheel. Despite the couple hours of sleep last night, she was still bone-tired. Caffeine helped. Some. But she needed an IV of dark roast if she wanted to be alert and awake for the rest of the day.

"You make a good point," she finally said to Dalton.

"My apartment might be the safest place for us right now," he said.

That was true for them and everyone around them.

"I'm coming with you," Jules said.

"Your plate is full already, taking care of Toby while being here for our grandparents," Dalton said. "Grandpa Lor is awake now. He'll need your support even more."

Jules opened her mouth to speak but then clamped down on her bottom lip instead.

"I'll have your truck swept before the two of you leave," Jules said. "Are you sure it's safe to go to your apartment? Because I can arrange a safe house to get you by until this blows over."

Going to an unfamiliar place where there would be strangers didn't exactly feel warm and fuzzy to Blakely. Not being able to go pick up Chase when she desperately wanted to be there for him was the hardest thing. Not being there for Bethany made her want to scream. What choice did she have? "It's hard to kill someone you can't find."

Jules looked to Dalton, who gave a slight nod.

Okay, then. They were going to a safe house.

"I can get you near Houston," Jules said as she retrieved her phone from her handbag. "How do you feel about Galveston?"

"Good," Dalton answered.

"Okay, then I think I have a place for you to hang out that should keep you off the radar," Jules said.

"While you're getting a sweep done on my truck, maybe I can take one of the ranch vehicles instead," Dalton said.

"No one should be expecting it," Jules said. "Give me half an hour, and I'll set everything up. In the meantime, dear brother, make sure you get clearance from the doctor to leave. Okay?"

He saluted. "Yes, ma'am."

The next hour was a blur of activity as Dalton cleaned up and got dressed, nurses scrambled around getting him ready for release, and a doctor was summoned to give the final okay for him to be discharged. He'd been clear about his intention to walk out with or without the doctor's permission. Waiting would get him in the least amount of trouble with his boss.

An apartment at The Waterfront on Bayou Shore Drive was arranged, and a ranch vehicle was parked at the side of the hospital. Jules would oversee the bomb sweep of Dalton's truck, drawing attention there while he and Blakely slipped out the side door and to the waiting vehicle.

Dalton stared at his cell. "Johnny Spear has been arrested at Lake Texoma, where he was hiding in a fishing cabin with no contact to the outside world."

"I'd started to move on from him as a suspect anyway," Blakely admitted. "It's good to know that I'm on the right track."

"Have you considered the professor?" Dalton asked before they were interrupted by a thumbs-up from Jules. "Go time."

Within a matter of minutes, they were racing down a staircase before hitting the side exit. An older gentleman scooted over to the passenger seat before exiting the truck with the engine left running.

"Shiloh Nash has worked the ranch since long before I was a twinkle in my parents' eyes. Grandpa Lor hired him at fifteen, and he's been there ever since," Dalton explained as Blakely crouched low in the seat. "Folks say all he needs to do is put his hands on a horse to hear its thoughts."

Despite his age, the man looked strong. He still had a full head of white hair.

"Sounds like he has a gift," she said, checking the side mirror to see if anyone was paying attention to them or if a vehicle was following them. So far, so good. Did she dare hope they would make it to Galveston?

"He's quite the character too," Dalton supplied. It was nice to talk about something so normal for a change.

"I wish we could stay here so you could have more time with your grandparents," she said.

Dalton tightened his grip on the steering wheel and kept his eyes on the patch of road in front of them. "They have Jules. Grandpa Lor is awake. Now we just need miracle number two."

Blakely could use one of those miracles about now.

THE DRIVE TO Galveston was quiet. They only made a lunch stop, eating fast food in the truck while parked across the street from the taco place. Apartment 4D of The Waterfront luxury apartments afforded a view of the Gulf of Mexico that Dalton might have appreciated more if he was on vacation. As it was, he checked the one-bedroom along with the perimeter with a wary eye. Once he deemed it safe, he joined Blakely inside, where she was rummaging around in the fridge.

"I meant to ask more about your relationship with the professor," he said to her.

"What relationship?" she asked.

"He shows up in your courtroom. Keeps track of your schedule. Surely you don't think it's for professional reasons only."

"He has a reputation for liking busty blondes, which I am not," she said, a little too quickly to dismiss his concerns. The guy did exhibit a stalker quality. "I admit he's made me uncomfortable on a couple of occasions, but I choose not to read too much into our interactions." She pulled out ingredients to make sandwiches. "I can also admit that seeing him in my courtroom yesterday was uncomfortable. Though, it wasn't the first time he's brought students." She closed the fridge door. "Do you see him as a threat?"

"I don't like his fixation on you," he admitted. "Has he ever made an advance?"

"I've been very clear where I stand with the professor," she said as she assembled dinner. Didn't mean the professor was on board or that he didn't resent her for refusing him. Would he resent her enough to come for her?

Dalton sent a message to Jules to see if she could pull up any dirt on the professor, like sexual harassment claims by current or former students. Any indications of escalation of stalking behavior.

He received an immediate response that Jules was on it.

After a quiet dinner, Blakely excused herself to take a shower. Dalton sat at the table and stared out the window. Now that Johnny Spear had been eliminated as a possibility, they were back to square one. The professor bugged Dalton. The man's actions raised red flags. Did it mean he was a murderer? Was he trying to scare Blakely? Get her to run to him in some twisted scenario in the man's mind?

Would he hire someone to hurt her? Abduct her?

It didn't add up.

Blakely's cell buzzed. Dalton resisted the temptation to check the screen. She would be out of the shower in a few minutes and could see for herself.

The darn thing barely stopped buzzing before kicking off a new round. An emergency?

He got to his feet and moved to the counter to check the screen. If he was going to read the messages, he needed her facial ID.

Since this seemed important, he picked up the phone and took it to the bathroom with him. Standing in the hallway, he knocked on the door as the cell went off again. "Sorry to interrupt, but your cell isn't letting up. Someone must want to get a hold of you desperately."

The water turned off.

A few seconds later, the door cracked enough for him to slip her phone through.

"Everything okay?"

"It's my sister," Blakely said. "She wants me to pick her up. Says she is being discharged first thing in the morning but doesn't want to go home and doesn't want anyone to realize she left the hospital in the middle of the night."

A minute later, she emerged from the bathroom dressed and still dripping wet.

"What should I do, Dalton?"

Hiding was going to drive Blakely out of her mind. Doing nothing was the absolute worst. "Tell me what to do because I can't leave my family hanging like this. There has never been a time when I wasn't there for them."

Dalton raked his fingers through his hair. "How tired are you?"

"I'm wide awake now," she admitted.

"Let's go get Bethany."

"How?" Did she dare hope he had a plan? Could they grab Bethany and bring her back to Galveston with them to hide out for a few days? What would that do to Chase? *Chase*.

"We'll figure it out on the drive over," he said.

"I'll grab clothes for her," Blakely said before throwing another jogging suit in her handbag along with the only other shoes she could find, ballet flats she'd packed.

Within a matter of minutes, they were back on the road.

The drive didn't take long at night with no traffic.

"You're authorized to go in the room, so maybe we arrange a swap while the nurses aren't looking?" Dalton asked after parking in the lot.

It could work. "I can change clothes with Bethany, and then she can walk out with you."

"We'll pretend to be a couple so I can hide her face," he added. It was cover, so the idea shouldn't bother her as much as it did.

"And then, I'll come out and say goodbye," she said. "Make a show of them seeing my face so they won't suspect anything."

"As busy as the nursing staff is, we have a good chance a different one will be at the station if we hold off for a few minutes," he reasoned. Someone was always at the station, but the nurses moved in and out of rooms.

"Let's do this."

Chapter Twenty-Four

The first part of the mission was a success. Dalton and Bethany waited in the parking lot. Now all Blakely had to do was give it a few minutes, and she could make her exit.

The sound of feet shuffling outside of her door sent her pulse flying. She climbed into bed, turned away from the door and pretended to be asleep. She forgot how often nurses came in and checked on patients. Bethany had complained about getting no sleep while in the hospital after having Chase.

This was so not good. Could she reach for her cell without drawing attention?

Footsteps sounded after the door was closed. The nurse was inside the room.

Hold on.

Something was off.

Would a nurse close the door behind her after entering the room?

No.

Someone was here.

Dalton would have made his presence known.

Squinting, she searched for something to use as a weapon on the nightstand next to the bed.

"You just won't die," came a growl from the familiar voice. A jolt of shock rocketed through her. A *whoosh* sound filled her ears as panic gripped her. Now she knew who was behind the attempts to kill her. And she couldn't believe who it was.

Blakely stayed quiet. She couldn't reach for the vase on the table without being caught. The voice was too close. Her heart pounded the inside of her ribcage. She could only hope the bastard couldn't hear it.

White-hot anger filled her as she clenched her fists. How could he?

As he came close enough for her to hear his breath, she hit the call button and burst from the covers. "Greg! You sonofabitch! I'm not Bethany."

He dove for her, ramming her in her midsection as voices sounded in the hallway. She crashed into the nightstand, cracking her head against the hard wood. The vase tipped over, slamming into her head first and then the tile floor, where it burst.

"What the hell?" Dalton's voice cut through the room as the light flipped on.

A nurse rushed into the room beside him.

But it was too late. Greg had pinned her to the floor and had a piece of glass to her throat.

"Back up or I'll cut her carotid artery," Greg demanded. The wild look in his eyes said he was desperate and would kill her if need be, despite the look of apology he shot her. "This isn't supposed to happen this way." He rocked back and forth, his elbow jabbing her in the chest as he held her down.

"What then? What was your plan? Kill your sister-in-law? For what reason?" Then it dawned on her.

"You were a decoy," he said. "Bethany is the one who is supposed to die."

"For what reason?" Blakely asked, distracting Greg while

she prayed everyone else was coming up with a plan. "My sister has nothing to give."

"Life insurance," Bethany said from behind them. Her tone said he'd drained her of any love she might have had for him over the years. "You asked me to sign the policy that you took out a few months ago. If everyone thinks my sister is the real target, and I'm accidentally killed, you'll get to play the grieving husband role. Is the money for your mistress?"

"I didn't... I don't..." Greg stuttered.

"Was I that awful of a wife that you wanted me gone? Dead?" Bethany asked. Now Blakely could hear the hurt.

If only she could somehow wiggle free or get hold of a piece of the vase to turn the tables on Greg. Could she make a move without triggering him?

The desperate look in his eyes, his actions—this wasn't the Greg she'd once known. How could she have missed the signs of his mental decline?

Busy. Being busy was a lousy excuse, even if it was true.

"I owe people," Greg finally said. "And they're coming for me if I don't pay up. These aren't the kind of people who let missed payments go unnoticed."

"How is that possible?" Bethany asked.

"You have no idea what it's like to try to keep up your lifestyle," he practically spat out. "I tried to be a good husband. I worked but you were never satisfied." There was nothing but anger and accusation in his tone now. Like a teapot boiling over.

Blakely made eye contact with Dalton, who gave an almost imperceptible headshake. He didn't want her to make a move.

Could she buck Greg off without causing him to slice her throat?

"You. You wanted the world handed to you on a silver platter." Greg's voice was almost hysterical now. "And you didn't care enough about me to see that I was drowning."

"Is this about your mother?" Bethany asked, panicked. "Because I tried to help with her when she was sick."

"She was all I had," Greg said.

"That's not true," Bethany argued. "You had me and you have a son. Remember Chase?"

Greg's wild eyes searched the room. "You'll never find him."

Oh. No.

"Did something happen to Chase?" Blakely managed to ask as Bethany's knees buckled and her legs came out from underneath her. Before she could hit the floor, Dalton scooped her up.

"I'm going to set her on the bed, okay, Greg?" he asked, taking a slow, measured step inside the room.

Greg's body stiffened. The sharp point pressed a little harder into Blakely's neck.

"Please, Greg," Blakely managed to say. "Don't do this. We'll get help for you. You still have a family." The thought this man could have hurt Chase had to be pushed out of her thoughts. She had to find a way to win him over. "We'll be there for you."

"Where have you been?" Greg asked. "You're just saying that now because you don't want to die."

"No, I don't," Blakely admitted as Dalton set Bethany on top of the covers.

"Back off," Greg said, his full attention on Dalton.

Could she make a move?

Distracted by Dalton, Greg released the pressure on her neck. It was now or never.

Blakely bucked. Greg lost his balance. He brought his

hand down to stabilize himself but ended up grabbing a handful of glass.

He bit out a string of curses as she rolled away, out of reach.

Dalton stepped in between them and drew his weapon. He identified himself to Greg and read the man his rights.

Bethany came to. "Where's Chase?"

"You'll never find him," Greg spit out as hospital security flooded the room. "He's gone."

Blakely felt sick. She grabbed her stomach as Bethany leaned over and threw up.

"No," her sister said. "You couldn't hurt our baby. Could you?"

Greg sneered as he was being placed into zip cuffs.

Please. Please. Please be bluffing.

"Where is he?" Bethany chanted as she managed to push off the bed and throw herself toward Greg. "I wasn't perfect, and neither were you. But Chase is innocent. He's just a boy."

Seeing her sister plead ripped Blakely's heart out.

"Let's go," she said to her sister. "We need to find Chase."

Dalton helped, asking security to have the police meet them at Bethany's home.

Fear and anger balled up together as Blakely managed to help her sister to the truck. A decoy. It made sense. The shot had come through the window after Blakely's attack.

Dalton drove like the street was on fire behind him. Blakely called out directions. Was the stranger who Greg had promised a payout to at Bethany's house right now? Did he have Chase? Or was Chase…

Blakely couldn't let herself think her nephew was gone.

All three of them flew out of the vehicle as Blakely fumbled for the key to unlock the door. All the lights were out.

From the outside, it looked like a normal home. What were they going to find inside?

Dalton took the lead, flipping on lights as they ran through the downstairs, checking rooms.

"Chase," Bethany called out.

A sleepy little boy appeared at the top of the stairwell.

"Mommy?" he asked, rubbing his eyes.

Despite everything she'd gone through physically, Bethany found a reserve of strength as she practically flew up the stairs. Adrenaline could do that to a person. Give them a burst of superhuman strength.

Dalton continued checking the home while Blakely joined her sister and nephew, wrapping them in a hug.

"Where's Daddy?" Chase asked.

"He's not coming home for a long time, baby," Bethany said. "But I'm here. I'm not going anywhere. Neither is your aunt Blakely."

"That's right, buddy," Blakely calmly reassured him.

Dalton joined them, cell to his ear. He said a few uh-huhs into the phone before thanking the caller and giving Bethany's address. "There's been an arrest. Kyle Newt is an ex-con who a certain person promised half the insurance money to for his help in removing a certain person from this life." He was intentionally speaking in vague terms that a seven-year-old wouldn't be able to follow. Greg might be a bastard for what he'd done, but he was still Chase's father. The boy would have to be protected as best as the family could.

Greg had been desperate. Desperate people did desperate things.

He was now a criminal.

"Are you coming home, Mommy?" Chase asked.

"What do you think about moving in with your aunt for a

little while?" Bethany asked before turning toward Blakely and whispering, "I don't think I can stay here."

"You'll live with me until you figure it all out," Blakely said.

Bethany wrapped her in a hug.

THE LAW HAD taken statements, and it was time to go home. Except Dalton had no idea where home was now. Because it felt a whole lot like Blakely.

"Are you leaving?" Blakely asked Dalton as Bethany pulled together a few items to take to her sister's house.

"I can drop you off at home if you'd like," he said.

"Here's the thing," Blakely said before capturing his gaze and holding on to it. "My definition of *home* has changed now that you came back into my life. In fact, it changed the weekend we spent in Galveston, but I was too scared to admit it."

"What are you saying?"

"That my home is here." She reached out and placed the flat of her palm on his heart. "If you'll let me back in, I promise to love you for the rest of my life."

Dalton covered her hand with his. "There's only one thing I've ever been certain of in my life and that's you. You are the only thing that makes sense. I'm in love with you, Blakely. But you need to know that I'm leaving my job to work the ranch full-time."

"Sounds like the perfect place to retreat to on the weekends if you ask me," she said without hesitation.

"Are you saying that you could see yourself splitting your time between the ranch and your home in Houston?" he asked for clarification.

"Only if you mean *our* home in Houston," she stated.

"I'm in love with you, Dalton. And I don't want to waste another day without you."

Dalton dropped down on one knee. "Then, I have a question to ask."

She brought her hand up to cover a gasp. When she removed it, all he saw was her beautiful smile.

"From the moment I met you, something inside me changed. Something clicked. And I know it sounds cliché, but I knew right then and there I was supposed to be with you for the rest of my life." He kissed her hand. "Would you do me the incredible honor of marrying me?"

"Yes," she said. "I'm so in love with you, Dalton, that it scared me. But I'm not afraid anymore. And I don't want to wait another day to make us official. I'll marry you any time, any place and any day."

Dalton stood up and hauled his fiancée against his chest, wrapping her in a warm embrace. "What are you doing tomorrow?"

"Marrying you," she said. Those words sent warmth spiraling through him. He dipped his head and claimed his fiancée's lips.

"One more thing," Dalton said. "What do you think about asking for a meeting with my mother?"

"If that's what you want, I'll be right by your side the whole time," she said. With her by his side, he felt like he could pull off anything.

"Do you think it's a good idea?"

"I think you won't know until you do it," she said before pressing a small kiss to his lips.

"Will you come with me?" he asked.

"Yes," she said. "From now on, you couldn't get rid of me if you tried."

"Good." Because he'd finally found home.

Dalton kissed Blakely tenderly at first and then hard, marking her as his as she did the same to him. One word came to mind…

Home.

* * * * *

Get up to 4 Free Books!

We'll send you 2 free books from each series you try PLUS a free Mystery Gift.

FREE Value Over **$25**

Both the **Harlequin Intrigue®** and **Harlequin® Romantic Suspense** series feature compelling novels filled with heart-racing action-packed romance that will keep you on the edge of your seat.

YES! Please send me 2 FREE novels from the Harlequin Intrigue or Harlequin Romantic Suspense series and my FREE gift (gift is worth about $10 retail). After receiving them, if I don't wish to receive any more books, I can return the shipping statement marked "cancel." If I don't cancel, I will receive 6 brand-new Harlequin Intrigue Larger-Print books every month and be billed just $7.19 each in the U.S. or $7.99 each in Canada, or 4 brand-new Harlequin Romantic Suspense books every month and be billed just $6.39 each in the U.S. or $7.19 each in Canada, a savings of 20% off the cover price. It's quite a bargain! Shipping and handling is just 50¢ per book in the U.S. and $1.25 per book in Canada.* I understand that accepting the 2 free books and gift places me under no obligation to buy anything. I can always return a shipment and cancel at any time by calling the number below. The free books and gift are mine to keep no matter what I decide.

Choose one:
- ☐ **Harlequin Intrigue Larger-Print** (199/399 BPA G36Y)
- ☐ **Harlequin Romantic Suspense** (240/340 BPA G36Y)
- ☐ **Or Try Both!** (199/399 & 240/340 BPA G36Z)

Name (please print)

Address   Apt. #

City   State/Province   Zip/Postal Code

Email: Please check this box ☐ if you would like to receive newsletters and promotional emails from Harlequin Enterprises ULC and its affiliates. You can unsubscribe anytime.

Mail to the Harlequin Reader Service:
IN U.S.A.: P.O. Box 1341, Buffalo, NY 14240-8531
IN CANADA: P.O. Box 603, Fort Erie, Ontario L2A 5X3

Want to explore our other series or interested in ebooks? Visit www.ReaderService.com or call 1-800-873-8635.

---

*Terms and prices subject to change without notice. Prices do not include sales taxes, which will be charged (if applicable) based on your state or country of residence. Canadian residents will be charged applicable taxes. Offer not valid in Quebec. This offer is limited to one order per household. Books received may not be as shown. Not valid for current subscribers to the Harlequin Intrigue or Harlequin Romantic Suspense series. All orders subject to approval. Credit or debit balances in a customer's account(s) may be offset by any other outstanding balance owed by or to the customer. Please allow 4 to 6 weeks for delivery. Offer available while quantities last.

Your Privacy—Your information is being collected by Harlequin Enterprises ULC, operating as Harlequin Reader Service. For a complete summary of the information we collect, how we use this information and to whom it is disclosed, please visit our privacy notice located at https://corporate.harlequin.com/privacy-notice. Notice to California Residents – Under California law, you have specific rights to control and access your data. For more information on these rights and how to exercise them, visit https://corporate.harlequin.com/california-privacy. For additional information for residents of other U.S. states that provide their residents with certain rights with respect to personal data, visit https://corporate.harlequin.com/other-state-residents-privacy-rights/.

HIHRS25